HEARTSEASE

THE CHANGES TRILOGY
by Peter Dickinson

The Devil's Children

Heartsease

The Weathermonger

HEARTSEASE

The Changes: Book Two

by Peter Dickinson

DELACORTE PRESS / NEW YORK

Published by
Delacorte Press
1 Dag Hammarskjold Plaza
New York, New York 10017

Chapter Decorations by Leo and Diane Dillon

MANUFACTURED IN THE UNITED STATES OF AMERICA

FIRST PRINTING

LIBRARY OF CONGRESS CATALOGING-IN-PUBLICATION DATA

Dickinson, Peter [date of birth].
Heartsease.
"The Changes—book 2."
Summary: At a future time in England when anyone
knowledgeable about machines is severely punished as
a witch, four children dare to aid in the escape of a
"witch" left for dead.
[1. Science fiction]   I. Title.
PZ7.D562He   1986   [Fic]   85-16179
ISBN 0-385-29451-4

for Philippa and Polly

Four Years Before . . .

The tunnel is dark and clammy, raw earth crudely propped. Bent double under its low roof an elderly man jabs with his crowbar at the work-face, levers loose earth away, rests panting for several heartbeats and then jabs again. This time the crowbar strikes a hard surface just below the earth. He mutters and tries again, jabbing in different places, only to find each time the same smooth hardness blocking his path, sloping upward away from him. Wearily he fetches a camper's gas lamp and peers at the obstacle, picking loose earth away from it with shaking fingers, and muttering to himself all the time. Suddenly he bends closer, pursing his lips, and runs a torn thumbnail down a crack in the smooth surface. The crack goes straight as a ruler, and meets the edge of the slab at an exact right angle. It is not natural rock, but stone measured and cut by masons.

His heart, which a moment before had been thudding with exhaustion, is now thudding with excitement. But he is a tidy-minded man and works methodically to clear a whole slab, and then to find leverage under it for his crowbar. Several hours pass, but at last he settles the steel into a crevice and leans his weight on it. The stone groans as it lifts. The man has a pebble ready to wedge the slit open. As he steps back to rest from that first effort he knocks his lamp over. In the new dark he sees that the slit is glowing, with a pale faint light, like a watch-dial. Something else. He does not see it, but feels it. Beyond the stone slab a Power lies.

So The Changes begin.

In that one night, all over Britain, the link between Man and Machine snapped.

On roads and motorways drivers forgot their skill and sat helpless while their cars or trucks hurtled off the tarmac. In factories the night shifts rioted and smashed. At Port Talbot a freak storm gathered and raged above the steel works until the lightning made the whole huge complex a destroying furnace. In ordinary houses, as dawn came on, the alarm clocks rang and sleepers woke to stare at the horrible thing clanging beside them. Some hands, out of sheer muscular habit, reached out for the lightswitch, only to snatch themselves back as though the touch of plastic stung like acid.

Day after day followed of panic and rumor. Cities began to burn, amid looting and riot. Then the main flights started, hundreds of thousands of people streaming away from their homes to look for food, safety, peace. Britain closed in on itself, like an anemone in a rock pool closing at a touch. When other nations tried to probe into the island, the island seemed to grow a mysterious wall around it. It was very difficult to get even a single spy through.

But behind the wall we began to change. The Changes were mostly inside us, in our minds, but a few were outside. In a bare hill valley a great oakwood grew, overnight, with a tower in the middle of it. A wild preacher, cursing the passersby for their sins, found he had called down a thunderstorm by accident. Soon others learned to do the same.

Men lived by rumor. Events in the next county became strange and far away. One winter, for instance, it was said in Yorkshire that dragons had begun to stir in the Pennine hills; quite sensible farmers took to sleeping with buckets of water beside their beds, ready to quench the fiery breath.

Most of the customs that grew up were concerned with witch-craft (as the use of machines was called). These also varied from shire to shire. Hereford, for instance, was very little troubled by witches and the reason for this (men believed) was the great Hereford Flower Dance, which lasted for fourteen days in May and was a time of singing and happiness, a celebration of the power of Nature against the horror of engines.

By contrast there were the great witch-findings in Durham Cathedral, with three thousand people massed under the frowning Norman arches, pale-cheeked and sweating, groaning all together as name after name was called, neighbors and wives and sons and cronies, to stand the unappealable tests.

In an island like this, so secretive, so unpredictable, how could a spy from the outside world survive? As he set up his little transmitter in a Cotswold copse, working with difficulty because the controls and connections seemed suddenly unfamiliar and awkward, how could he know that he would be smelled out, ambushed, seized and stunned, and then wake to find his legs shackled by oak stocks, his back against a wall, and himself facing a baying crowd of villagers? And then the brief, jeering trial and the hail of stones . . .

CONTENTS

1 The Stones Are Burning   15

2 Dog Pack   35

3 There's Wickedness About   61

4 First Snow   89

5 We Need a Bomb   110

6 Will She Go?   135

7 Engines   153

8 Knife and Rope   177

9 Wild Water   199

10 And Home . . .   223

   And After . . .   234

HEARTSEASE

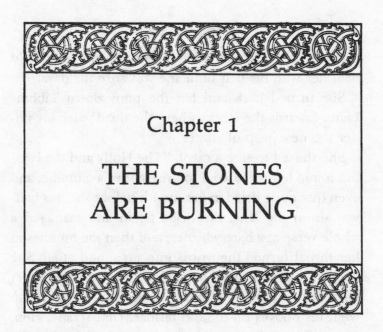

Chapter 1

THE STONES ARE BURNING

It was the last of the soft days of autumn. As dusk fell, you could feel the frosts coming, a smell of steel in the air.

If it hadn't been so nearly dark Margaret would have gone the long way around; but she was tired and Scrub was even tireder, his head drooping, his mane clotted with sweat, his hooves not making their proper clipclop, but muddling the sound with a scrapy noise because he wasn't lifting them up properly. Even so she began to lead him the long way, without thinking about it. It was only the clank of a milking bucket from Fatchet's cowshed reminded her that Uncle Peter would be finished milking soon; if she came back after he'd sat down in his rocking chair in the farm kitchen and begun to drink his evening's cider from the big blue-and-white mug, he'd beat her with his belt until she was sore for days.

She turned back and led the pony down Tibbins Lane, towards the stocks where the dead witch lay under the new heap of stones.

She started to sing a carol, "The Holly and the Ivy," but found her voice wouldn't rise above a mumble, and even that noise dried in her mouth before she was halfway down the lane. She tried again and managed a whole verse at a bare whisper, and then the muscles in her throat turned the words into no sound at all. She would have run if she'd been alone, but Scrub was past anything except his dragging walk. Clip, scrape, clop went his hooves on the old tarmac, clip, scrape, clop. She could see the heap of stones now, lying against the Rectory wall as though they'd just been tipped from a cart—not brought in baskets and barrows by a hundred villagers for throwing.

All at once she thought of Jonathan; just like him to be helping Aunt Anne with the baking that morning, so that he hadn't been made to go and watch the stoning. He'd laugh at her, his sharp snorting laugh, if she told him she'd ridden so far to get away from this heap of stones that now she had to come back right past it. Jonathan always thought things out before he did them. Come on, Margaret, it's only a heap of stones and what's left of a foreign witch. Come on.

As she passed the neat pile the stones groaned.

Margaret dropped the reins and ran. Forty yards on, where the walls narrowed into an alleyway between two cottages, she waited, panting, for Scrub. He clopped down in the near-dark and nuzzled against her shoulder, but nothing else moved in the dusk behind him.

Uncle Peter was still whistling shrilly at his milking stool when she led the pony past the cowshed toward the little paddock which he shared with poor neglected Caesar. Jonathan was waiting for her, leaning against the pillar of the log-store, his little pointed face just like a gnome's under his shaggy black hair.

"What's wrong, Marge?" he said.

"Nothing."

"Is it to do with the witch? You didn't watch, did you?"

"No, of course not."

"But it is, isn't it?"

"Oh, Jo, it was . . . I had to come back down Tibbins Lane because I was so late, and when I passed him he groaned. I thought witches died, just like anybody else."

Jonathan tilted his head over the other way, still watching her with his bright, strange eyes—like a bird deciding whether to come for the crumbs you are holding in the palm of your hand.

"You're not making this up, are you, Marge?"

"No, of course not!"

"All right. Now listen. I'll take Scrub out and put his harness away. You—"

"But why?"

"Listen! You go and offer to carry one of Father's buckets in—he won't let you, but it'll tell him you're

home. Go and say hello to Mother, then go upstairs
noisily and quietly into my room. Climb out along the
shed roof and jump down into the old hay. I'll meet you
there."

"But why, Jo?"

"Because he's still alive, of course. We've got to get
him out. Tim'll help us, but we'll need you too."

"Jo, you'll—"

"Yes, I'll take care of your precious Scrub. Go slowly,
Marge. Talk slowly. Try and sound just tired, and nothing else."

She gave him the reins, started to walk toward the
cowshed door, turned back to shout to him to see that
there was enough water in the trough, realized that it
would be dangerous to shout (dangerous now, in a
house which was safe this morning) and walked on.

Uncle Peter was milking Florence, so he must be
almost finished. There were two full buckets by the
door, so he'd be middling pleased—last week he hadn't
managed to fill even two most days.

"Can I carry one of these in for you, Uncle Peter?"

He grunted but didn't look up. "You leave 'em be,"
he said. "Too heavy for a slip like you, Marge. Where
you been all day, then?"

"Riding."

"Long ride. Didn't you fancy what we did to that
foreigner this morning?"

Margaret said nothing.

"Ach, don't you be feared to tell *me*. You're a good
lass, Marge, and I wouldn't have you hard-hearted, but

you must understand that it's necessary. Thou shalt not suffer a witch to live, the Book says. Look now, I took nigh on half a bucket out of Maisie, who was dry as an old carrot till this very day, when she should by all rights have been flowing with milk like the land of Canaan—what was that but witchcraft?"

"I suppose you're right, Uncle Peter."

"Course I am, girl. You go in now. You'll have forgot all about it by tomorrow."

Aunt Anne was in the kitchen, which had been the living room before the Changes came. She was rocking her chair an inch to and fro in front of the bread-oven, staring at nothing, her face drawn down into deep lines as though she wanted to cry but couldn't. Margaret said hello but she didn't answer, so it seemed best to go thumpingly up the stairs, tiptoe into Jonathan's room, wriggle out through his window and crawl down the edge of the shed where the tiles were less likely to break.

The hay was last year's, gray with mustiness, but thick enough to break a clumsy jump. She picked herself up and moved into the shadow of a stack of bean poles which Uncle Peter had leaned against the shed wall. It really was night now, with a half-moon coming and going behind slow-moving clouds, and the air chill for waiting in; but before she began to feel cold inside herself she heard a low bubbling sound which meant that Tim was coming up the path from his hut in the orchard. The moon edged out as he reached the shed, and she saw that he was carrying a sheep hurdle under

one arm and a full sack on his other shoulder. Jonathan
was with him.

"You there, Marge?" he whispered. "Good. Hold
this. I won't be long."

He handed her a saw and scampered off down the
path. Tim at once began to make his bubbling noise
more loudly, because Jonathan was the only person he
knew and trusted, apart from his own sister, Lucy.
Other people teased him and threw things at him, or
were frightened of him and kept away; but inside his
poor muddled brain he knew that Jonathan really
thought of him as a person, and not as an animal who
happened to be shaped like a man.

"It's all right, Tim," whispered Margaret, speaking as
she might have done to Scrub, "he's coming back. Be
brave." The whisper seemed to make Tim feel he was
with someone who wouldn't hurt him, so he settled
down to wait and the bubbling quietened in his throat.
Jonathan was away several minutes, and when he came
back he walked slowly, bent sideways by the weight of
the heavy thing he was carrying.

"What's that?" said Margaret.

"Petrol, I think. It burns. I found a few tins hidden
under the straw in the old barn where the machines
are."

"But you aren't allowed to go there!" whispered
Margaret.

"Tim can carry it," said Jonathan. "And the sack.
There won't be anyone in the road now it's really dark.
I'll manage the hurdle and you take the saw, Marge.

Keep in the shadows. If someone does come, stand still until you're sure they've seen you. If you have to run away, don't drop the saw or they'll know where it came from. Climb up the ivy on the other side of this wall and you can get back onto the roof. Off we go."

Tim followed him like a dog at its master's heels. The alley between the cottages was a black canyon, but beyond it the moon shone clear against the Rectory wall. Tim moved more quietly than the children because he didn't have proper shoes, not even clogs; his feet were wrapped in straw which he tied into place with strips of old rag. The stocks had been set opposite the gate into Squire's house, where the road was wider, so that there would be plenty of room for the villagers to gather round and throw things at whoever was in them—soft fruit and rotten eggs and clods of turf at ordinary bad people, stones at witches.

The pile was silent now, but Jonathan didn't stop to listen to it. He started lifting the stones away, not dropping them but putting them down carefully so as not to make any noise. Tim watched, bubbling quietly, and then began to help. When Margaret lifted her first stone the witch groaned again.

There weren't as many stones as there seemed. The pile looked big because Mr. Gordon, the fierce old sexton, had made the men pick the loose ones up when the stoning was over and heap them into a neat cairn. Before long Margaret tried to pull a bigger stone out but found it was soft and warm—a legging with a leg inside it. In a few minutes more they had cleared the legs up as far as the stocks.

"You two carry on with the top half," said Jonathan, "while I cut through here."

"But Jo," whispered Margaret, "won't they start hunting for him when they see it's sawn through? They'll know someone's got him out."

"That's what the petrol's for."

He was already sawing, slowly but firmly, making as little noise as possible. Margaret and Tim labored on, lift, stoop, lift, stoop, lift, stoop. No single stone seemed to make the cairn any smaller, but soon they had cleared the body up to the waist. Tim had stopped his bubbling and was working with increasing urgency now that he could see enough of the witch's body to know what it was; he cooed once or twice, a noise which Margaret hadn't heard him make before. The witch had sheltered his head behind crooked arms, but these were now stuck to the mess of clotted blood and clothing and hair around his face; when Margaret tried to move an arm to get at a stone which had lodged in the bend of the elbow he groaned with a new, sharp note.

"He ought to be dead," whispered Jonathan. "Perhaps he's wearing some kind of armor under his clothes."

Tim knelt down beside the bloodied head and with slow tenderness, cooing like a distant pigeon in June, lifted the wincing tangle and cradled it against his dirty chest while Margaret picked out the last stone and eased the arms down into the man's lap. Jonathan sawed with even strokes, as though he was in no hurry at all.

"Oak," he whispered. "About three minutes more. Watch out up the lane, Marge, just in case."

The last tough sliver gave beneath the sawteeth and he lifted the imprisoning timber from the man's ankles. Then he fetched the hurdle and laid it beside the body. Tim, without being told, eased the wounded man on.

"We'll each take a corner in front, Marge. Tim can carry the back."

The weight was heavy but manageable. As soon as they were well clear of the rubble Jonathan lowered his corner to the ground so that Margaret and Tim had to do so too. Then he tipped the contents of the sack out and arranged them carefully around the stocks—straw and kindling and a few small pieces of plank. He opened the can and poured its contents over his bonfire and the surrounding stones. An extraordinary smell rose into the night air, and all at once Margaret remembered the seaside, which she'd completely forgotten about for five years—a smooth sea, hot sun, sand crawling with people, and behind it all a road where just such a smell came from, because a lot of machines were waiting there for three ladies in white coats to—she remembered the right words—fill them up. She hadn't thought of petrol, or the sea, or machines as things which took you to places, for ages—not since she was how old? The Changes were five years back, she and Jonathan were fourteen now, so not since she was nine.

Now this smell, sharp, rather nasty, filling your nose like chopped onions, brought all the pictures back.

"We'll let it soak while we get him down to the barn," whispered Jonathan. "I'll come back with a lantern to light it. People will run out if they see the flames now."

"Why do you want to burn the stocks?" said Margaret as she picked up her corner of the hurdle.

"Burn the saw marks. Then people might think he got away by witchcraft."

They didn't talk again as they carried the witch through the alley, along the stretch of road at the bottom, down through the farm gate and yard and along the steep path behind the pigsties to the big barn where the wicked machines stood in their rusting rows. Jonathan seemed to know his way about and led them unstumbling through the blackness to a place where there was a little hut inside the barn. He pushed a door open, and another forgotten smell lifted out into the night, more oily than petroly this time.

"I think he'll be safe here," he said. "There's a big engine without wheels in the middle; I don't know what it was for but it drove a big fan and pushed air into those towers outside. Marge, you'll have to climb up the ivy to my room and get some coverings to keep him warm. Straw, Tim. Straw. Straw. Good boy."

Tim bubbled his understanding and slouched out. Jonathan was shuffling around in the blackness, making a sweeping noise. Margaret waited, jobless, to help shift the witch. Then the faint square of lighter blackness in the doorway was blocked and she could smell fresh straw—Tim must have robbed the stack by the pigsties.

"I've cleared a place here," said Jonathan. "Hurry, Marge—we can move him."

The ivy was harder to climb than Jonathan had implied, but she managed it on the third go. She whisked the blankets off his bed, threw them out of the window, and went slowly down the stairs. Aunt Anne was still sitting in tragic stillness by the ovens, but this time she looked up when Margaret came in.

"Pete should be back in ten minutes," she said. "He's talking to Mr. Gordon. You must be hungry after all that riding—there's mutton and bread in the larder if you want something to keep you going."

"Oh, yes, please," said Margaret. "I've just remembered I didn't check whether the ponies had enough water. I won't be out long."

She found what she wanted in the larder: two fresh rolls, apples, slices of mutton, and one of the little bottles of cordial which Aunt Anne had brewed last March. She took the bottle from the back of the shelf and hoped it wouldn't be missed. As she was going out through the porch she had another thought and picked up one of the half-dozen lanterns which were always there. Aunt Anne didn't even move her eyes when she crossed the kitchen and lit the wick with a spill from the fire. Jonathan met her just outside the porch.

"Bit of luck," he whispered. "I thought I'd have to sneak in to light mine. Put it down—I've got a bit of dry straw. Shield the light as you go down the path, Marge."

He knelt in the moonlight and flipped the little doors open; deft and sure he lit his straw and moved the quick flame into the other lantern in time to light the wick before the straw was all burned. Margaret carried her lantern around the corner of the house where the pile of bedding lay, picked the blankets up and hid its light among them.

The witch was moaning on his straw. His face in the yellow lantern light was an ugly mess of raw flesh, his lips fat with bruising, his eyes too puffy to open. Margaret tucked her blankets around him, put the food where he could reach it, opened the bottle and tried to push its neck between his lips. With a jerky movement the man's hand came up and grabbed at the bottle, tilting it up until the yellow stuff was pouring out of the corners of the hurt mouth. He swallowed four times and then let his hand fall so that Margaret had to snatch at the bottle to prevent it from spilling all over him.

"Thanks," he whispered.

She started to sponge the cordial from his jaw with a corner of her skirt, but stopped in a welter of panic—someone was moving out in the barn. She knelt, quite still, then realized that the lantern was more betraying than any movement—rats scuttle, but they don't send out a steady gold glow. As she was moving to blow it out she heard the man in the barn make a different noise, a faint bubbling, Tim.

The big zany shambled through the door, carrying more straw and an indescribable mixture of old rags. He walked toward the wounded witch as if he was going to dump his load on him, then stopped. He stared at the blankets, then at the lantern, then at Margaret. Then he cooed and added a quiet little cluck of satisfaction before he took his bundle over to another corner of the hut and began to spread it about. Margaret realized that he'd brought his own bedding to keep the wounded witch warm, and now he intended to spend the night there to look after him. She decided to leave the lantern; Lucy was such a lazy slut that she'd never notice there was one missing when she cleaned and filled them in the morning.

As she stood up she looked for the first time at the other thing in the hut, the hulking old engine, bolted down into the concrete floor, streaked orange and black with dribbles of rust and the ooze of oil. She fitted her lantern into a nook where a lot of pipes masked it from three sides, in case there were cracks in the outside wall where the light could shine through and betray them. Then she left.

Uncle Peter was in his chair, and Aunt Anne and Lucy were putting supper out on the table, home bread and boiled mutton and turnips. The steamy richness filled the kitchen.

"Where you been, Marge?" he said.

"I'd forgotten to see if there was enough water for the ponies."

"Good lass, but I can't have you traipsing about the farm at all hours of darkness. You must learn to do things while it's still daylight. But never mind this time. Where's that son of mine, though?"

Feet clattered on the stairs and Jonathan rushed into the room, flushed and bright-eyed.

"Sorry I'm late," he said, "but I was looking out of my window and a great big fire started up suddenly in the lane. It doesn't look like an ordinary fire. One minute there wasn't anything, then it was like sunrise. What do you think's happening?"

Uncle Peter jumped to his feet, picked his cloak off the settle and his cudgel from behind the door, and strode growling out. Aunt Anne stood with the ladle in one hand, the other clutching the back of a chair, her face as gray as porridge. Then she sighed, shrugged, and began to spoon meat and gravy and turnips into bowls. Lucy took the big cleaving knife and hacked off clumsy chunks of bread, which she handed around. Aunt Anne mumbled a quick grace and they sat down.

At once Jonathan was talking about a bird he'd seen that afternoon, which he thought might be a harrier. He held a piece of mutton on the point of his knife and waved it over the table to show how the bird had spiraled up out of the valley; then he popped the meat into his neat little mouth (which looked too small to take it) and settled down to chewing. Nobody else said anything. Margaret knew that she ought to be hungry after all that misery and riding and excitement, but the excitement was still buzzing in her, making her blood run too fast through her veins to allow it to settle down to anything so stolid and everyday as eating and digesting. She dipped a morsel of bread into gravy and watched the brown juice soak up through its cells; she ate that slowly, and then picked up the smallest piece of meat on her plate with the point of her knife and managed to swallow that too. Lucy had gobbled, and was already giving herself a second helping. Aunt Anne ate almost nothing.

After twenty minutes Uncle Peter flung through the door, his cheeks crimson above his beard. He tossed his cudgel into the corner.

"Gone!" he cried.

"Gone?" said Aunt Anne, shrilly.

"Gone to his master the Devil!" shouted Uncle Peter. "I tell you, the stones were burning!"

"What does that mean?" said Jonathan in an interested voice.

"They were burning," said Uncle Peter solemnly. "Not much, by the time I came there, but I could see where they'd been blackened with big flames. And they weren't honest Christian flames, neither—the whole lane reeked of the Devil—the stink of wickedness—you know it when you smell it. And the little flames that were left, they were yellow but blue at the edges, not like mortal fire."

"Were the stocks all burned too?" said Margaret. Uncle Peter was too excited to notice how strained her voice came out, but Jonathan glanced sharply toward her.

"Burntest of all," said Uncle Peter. "Roaring and stinking still."

"Oh dear," said Aunt Anne. "I don't know what to think. We've kept your supper warm for you, Pete."

"We'll know tomorrow," said Uncle Peter, "when I've done milking Maisie. I reckon the witch has gone home to his master, and she'll be carrying a full bag."

He sat down and plunged into the business of eating, tearing off great hunks of bread and sloshing them around his platter before stuffing them into the red hole in the middle of his ginger beard, where the yellow teeth chomped and the throat golloped the lumps down. Margaret, who did not like to watch this process, looked away and her eye fell on Lucy. Lucy was a house servant, so she did not speak unless she was spoken to, though she sat at the same table with them all. (Where else was there for her to sit, if she wasn't to share a shed with her poor mad brother?) Now her black eyes sparkled above her plump red cheeks as she drank the excitement, looking from face to face; but the moment she saw Margaret watching her she dropped her glance demurely to the table. She was a funny secret person, Margaret thought, just as much a foreigner as the witch, really. Four years back she'd led Tim into the village— she'd been twelve then, she said, and Tim must have been about fifteen, but nobody knew for certain—and asked for shelter. They'd stayed ever since, but Margaret knew her no better than the day she came.

The moment Uncle Peter had speared his last chunk of mutton and thrust it into his mouth, Lucy was on her feet to take his plate and bring him the big round of cheese. He was swilling at his mug of rough cider when the door was racked with knocking. Aunt Anne started nervously to her feet and Uncle Peter shouted, "Come in!" It was Mr. Gordon, the sexton, his broad hat pulled down to hide most of his knobbly face, his shoulders hunched with rheumatism, but his blackthorn stick held forward in triumph like an emperor's staff.

"The Devil has taken his own!" he cried.

"Off to bed with you, children," said Aunt Anne, with a sudden echo of the brisk command she used to own before she became so silent. "I'll clear, thank you, Lucy."

Lucy curtsied and said good night in her soft voice and slipped up the stairs. Margaret kissed her aunt on the cheek, bobbed to her uncle and went too. Jonathan came last, and above the noise of his shoes on the bare stairs Margaret could hear Mr. Gordon and Uncle Peter settling down to excited talk over the meaning of the magical fire. As she undressed she saw how extraordinary it was that they shouldn't even think of petrol— they'd been grown men before the Changes. Then she remembered that she'd only found the picture of the seaside in a dark cranny at the back of her mind—a place which she knew she was supposed to keep shut, without ever having been told so. And Jonathan was a funny boy, treating the adventure so calmly, knowing just what to do all the time, thinking things out all the time behind his ugly little cat-face. He must have remembered about petrol and machines long ago, if he'd been exploring in the barn enough to know his way through it in the pitch dark.

She herself remembered about central heating as she rushed the last piece of undressing, wriggled into her flannel nightdress and jumped into bed. Once the house had been warm enough for her to open her presents on Christmas morning, wearing only her pajamas. Why . . .

She sat bolt upright in bed, knowing that if she asked that sort of question aloud Uncle Peter and Mr. Gordon and the others would be stoning *her* for a witch. She shivered, but not with cold this time, and blew out her candle. At once the horrible business of the morning floated up through her mind—the jostling onlookers, and the cheering, and the straining shoulders of the men as they poised their stones for throwing. She tried to shut it out, twice two is four and four is eight and eight is sixteen and sixteen is thirty-two and thirty-two is sixty-four and sixty-four is, is a hundred and twenty-eight and . . . but each time she got stuck the pictures came flooding back. She heard Mr. Gordon cackle exultantly from the door as he left, and Uncle Peter's booming good-nights. Still she lay, afraid to shut her eyes, staring through the diamond-paned window to where Orion was just lifting over the crest of Cranham woods.

Something scratched at the door.

"Who is it?" she croaked.

"Me," whispered Jonathan through the slight creak of the opening door. "I must oil that. Come and listen. Quietly."

She put on her cloak and tiptoed onto the landing. Flickering light came up the stairs as the fire spurted. Jonathan caught her by her elbow in the darkness.

"Stop there," he whispered. "The floor squeaks further on. You can hear from here."

Aunt Anne and Uncle Peter were still in the kitchen, arguing. Uncle Peter's voice was rumbly with cider and not always clear, but Aunt Anne's had a hysterical edge which carried every syllable up to the listeners.

"I tell you I can't stand it any longer," she was saying. "Everything that's happened is wicked, wicked! What harm had that poor man done us this morning, harm that you can prove, prove like you know that if you drop a stone it will fall? And forcing the children up there to see him die. I kept Jo back, and I'd do so again, but Marge is like a walking ghost. Oh, Pete, you must see, it can't be right to do that to children!"

"Rumble mumble Maisie nigh filled a bucket tonight when she was dry mumble rumble answer me that woman!"

"Oh, for God's sake, you know as well as I do that you've only just moved the cows down to the meadow pasture. They *always* make more milk the first couple of days there."

"Rumble bang shout off you go before I take my cudgel to you!"

A gulping noise. Aunt Anne was really crying now.

"Wouldn't she help?" whispered Margaret.

"She's too near breaking as it is," whispered Jonathan. "But Lucy will be useful."

"Lucy! But she's . . ."

"You've never even thought about her, Marge. Just look what she's managed for Tim. And anyway, Tim's deep in it, so she'll *have* to help. Thank you for asking about the stocks. Bed now."

This time Margaret found she could shut her eyes and there was a different picture in her mind: she'd reined Scrub up for a breather on the very top of the Beacon and looked northwest toward Wales. The limestone hill plunged at her feet toward the Vale; there lay the diminishing copses and farms, and beyond them the gray smudge which was the dead city of Gloucester, and beyond that, green so distant that it was almost the color of smoke—but through those far fields snaked the gleaming windings of the Severn toward, in the distant west (often you couldn't be sure whether what you were seeing was cloud or land or water, but today you could) the Bristol Channel. The sea.

Chapter 2

DOG PACK

The frosts came, and shriveled the last runner beans. Even at midday the air had a tang to it which meant that soon there would be real winter. Any wind made whirlpools of fallen leaves in odd corners.

It was three days before the witch spoke. To either of the children, that is—maybe he talked to Tim, but if so Tim couldn't tell them. And it was dangerous to go down much to the old tractor barn where the wicked machines stood.

"If you've got to go," said Jonathan, "look as if you're making for Tim's shed. Carry something he might need—food or an old rag. Then sneak round the back of the barn. And once you're past Tim's shed walk on a fresh bit of grass each time, or you'll make a path

and someone will spot it. You do realize we're stuck
with a dangerous job, Marge?"

"Stuck?"

"Well, wouldn't you rather you'd never heard him?
Rather someone else had? Then we could have rubbed
along as we were."

Margaret didn't know what she'd rather, so she
hadn't said anything. Next time she went to the barn
she carried a knuckle of mutton with a bit of meat still
on it, and actually walked into Tim's shed as if she was
going to leave it for him. She looked around at the
stinking heaps of straw, with the late-autumn flies haz-
ing about in the dimness, and wondered how she'd
never thought about the way Tim lived, any more than
she thought about the cows who came squelching
through the miry gates to milking. She'd thought far
more about Scrub than Tim.

Ashamed, she looked around the dank lean-to to find
something she could do now, at once, to make the zany
more comfortable. There was nothing, but in her
search she saw a triangular hole in the corrugated iron
which formed the back of the shed. And on the other
side of the hole was the wheel of a wicked machine, a
. . . a . . . a *tractor*. Of course, this shed was propped
against the back of the barn, and if the hole were larger
she could slip through to where the witch lay, and
there'd be no danger of leaving a track through the rank
grasses below the barn.

She tugged at the ragged edge of metal, and the
whole sheet gave and fell out on top of her. It left a hole

just like a door. Inside were the derelict machines and the little brick hut in the corner. And inside that were the rusting engine, Tim, and the witch. He looked a little better, but not enough; it was difficult to tell because of the deceiving yellow light from the lantern and because his face was still livid and puffy with bruising. Tim squatted in his corner of the shed, watching her as suspiciously as a bitch watches you when you come to inspect her puppies. Margaret took the bone to him, then knelt beside the witch. She'd brought a corner of fresh bread spread with cream cheese; she broke bits off and popped them into the smashed mouth whenever it opened—it was like feeding a nestling sparrow, except that nestlings are greedy. It took him a long time to chew each piece, and longer still to swallow.

"Looks to me as if he could do with a wash," said a soft voice.

Chill with terror Margaret swung around. Lucy was standing in the doorway, her hands on her hips, her face more foreign than ever—elfish, almost—in the faint light of the lantern. She wasn't looking at Margaret, but down at the wounded witch.

"Yeah," he said with a rasping sigh, "water would be good."

"But how are we going to get it here without anyone . . ." She stopped. In the panicky silence she could hear Tim gnawing a morsel of mutton out from a cranny of bone. She stood up, trying to seem (and feel) like a mistress talking to a servant.

"Lucy," she said hotly, "if you tell anyone . . ."

But Lucy was smiling, and Margaret could think of no threats that would mean anything.

"It's I could be menacing you, Miss Margaret, and not t'other way about. But I'll help you for Tim's sake. I mind him sitting by my bed when I had the measles, afore they took him away, just bubbling, but he made me feel better nor any of the medicines they gave me. He'd have been a doctor, Tim would, supposing he'd been in his right mind."

"Doctor?"

"Leech, then, but a proper un. I'll be fetching hot water. Fruit's what he needs, miss, not that pappy bread."

"What shall I do? Can I help?"

Lucy looked at her again—not her secret, half-mocking glance, but something new, considering, only a little suspicious.

"Aye," she said at last, "mebbe you could. We'll make as if we're mucking out Tim's shed, which I should a done weeks back. The Master's in Low Pasture, and your aunt's too fazed to notice what we do. So I'll go and set the big kettle on the stove, and you could mebbe fork all that straw out of Tim's shed and set light to it. Mind you don't burn his treasures—you'll find 'em under a bit of planking in the back corner."

She slipped out, silent as a stoat. Margaret had to run and scramble over the tow-bars in the dark barn to call after her in a straining whisper, "I'll come and help you with the kettle, Lucy."

Lucy turned, black in the bright rectangular gap

where the iron sheet had been, nodded in silence and flitted away.

There was a hayfork by the midden above the orchard. Margaret scrattled the straw in the shed together—it was cleaner than she'd thought, just musty with damp from the bare earth beneath; and really there were no more flies under the low roof than there were in any other shed on the farm. The plank in the corner she left where it was, after inquisitively lifting it to see what Tim's "treasures" were: a broken orange Dinky-toy earth-shifter; a plastic water pistol; the shiny top of a soda siphon; a child's watch which could never tell the time because the knob at the side only made the big and little hands move around the dial together. As she put the plank back Margaret was astonished that she should know what they all were—four days ago they would have been meaningless, except that she'd have known they were wicked.

She picked the driest straw she could see from her heap, twisted it together and took it back into the hut where the witch lay. Tim began to croak with alarm when she opened the lantern to poke it into the flame, so she carried the lantern out into the shed, lit her wisp of straw there and thrust it into the heap. After she'd put the lantern back she stood for several minutes leaning on her fork and watching the yellow stems shrivel into black threads which wriggled as the fire ate into the innards of the pile. Her cheeks were sharp with heat when she began to walk up through the orchard toward the house.

Lucy was in the kitchen, struggling to carry the
steaming kettle single-handed. Aunt Anne sat on one
side of the stove in an upright chair and Mr. Gordon sat
in the rocking chair between the stove and the fire,
rocking and clucking. Neither of them looked as though
they would pay any more attention to the comings and
goings of children than they did to the tortoiseshell
butterfly which pattered against the windowpane.

"Can I help you with that, Lucy?" said Margaret.

"If you please, Miss Margaret," said Lucy. "I thought
I'd best clean out Tim's shed afore winter sets in."

Margaret picked up a cloth and gripped one handle
of the kettle with it. But it wasn't a kettle, she thought. A
kettle was a small shiny thing with a cord going in at the
back. You didn't put it on the stove, but it got hot from
inside because the cord was . . . was electric. This big
pan they were edging out through the door, very carefully so that the hot water wouldn't slop over, was a
. . . a . . . preserving pan. She looked excitedly at
Lucy's down-bent face.

"I say, Lucy, I've just remembered . . ."

"Careful, Miss Margaret, or you'll be spilling it all,
and then we'll have our work wasted."

The interruption was soft and easy, but the glance
from under the little lace cap was as fierce as a branding
iron. Margaret suddenly saw what a comfortable time
she'd had of it since the Changes—Scrub to break and
ride and care for, a share of housework, only the occa-
sional belting from Uncle Peter to be afraid of. Wary, of
course, but never till now Lucy's cowering softness, like

the stillness of a mouse when a hawk crosses the sky above it. Not even Jonathan's dangerous adventuring.

Those times were over, since they'd rescued the witch. She would have to cower and adventure with the others. This was what Jonathan had meant about being stuck.

They could never have cleaned the witch without Tim. At first, while Lucy dabbed at the spoiled face, bristly with beard between the scabs, he squatted beside the bedding and watched with the soft glance of a clever spaniel. But as soon as they tried to lift their patient and undress him Tim pushed gently between them and ran his arm under the limp shoulders, lifting the body this way and that while the girls eased the torn and blood-clotted rags off.

"We'd best be burning most of this too," said Lucy. "D'you think you could find some old clothes of the Master's, Miss Margaret—nothing that he'll miss, mind?"

"I'll try," said Margaret. "Jo was right—he is wearing some kind of armor."

"Yeah," said the witch faintly. "Bulletproof, but not rockproof. I figure I got two or three busted ribs, and a busted arm, and I don't seem to move my legs like I used to. You some sort of resistance movement, huh?"

"Resistance?" said Margaret.

"I guessed . . ." said the witch, and paused. "Oh, forget it, you're only kids, anyway. Who knows I'm here?"

"Me and Jonathan and Lucy and Tim," said Marga-

ret. "I heard you groaning under the stones and I told
Jonathan and we got Tim to help us bring you down
here. Uncle Peter would kill you if he knew, though."

"Us too, mebbe," said Lucy, so softly that Margaret
only just caught the words. Then she added in a brisker
voice, "Which is your bad arm, mister?"

"Left. Roll me over on my right side and you can
unzip my armor."

They had to show Tim what they wanted, and he
turned the witch over as gently as a shepherd handling a
lamb. The man's legs flopped uncontrolledly, not
seeming to move properly with him, like a puppet's.
Then the zip puzzled them for a few seconds, but they
both remembered in the same instant and reached out
to pull the tag down.

"You'd best be looking for them clothes, Miss Margaret," chided Lucy. "If we let him chill off, he'll catch his
death, surely."

Margaret walked slowly up through the orchard,
coming to terms with this new Lucy, not the slut who
didn't fill the lamps or rake out the ashes or scrub the
step clean, but a different girl, a stranger, who knew just
what needed doing. Rather than risk Mr. Gordon's
fierce and knowing glance she climbed the ivy and
crawled in through Jonathan's window—much easier by
daylight than it had been in the dark. When she tiptoed
out onto the landing she saw Jonathan crouched at the
top of the stairs; he looked around at her and put his
finger to his lips.

"What's happening?" whispered Margaret.

He beckoned, then pointed to the floor; he must be showing her which board creaked, so she stepped over it and crouched by his side. He said nothing, but the steady clack of Mr. Gordon's rocking chair came up the stairs, mixed with his wheezing and clucking.

"He's waiting for her to break," whispered Jonathan at last. "I don't know what to do. He's willing her to it."

"Can you go in and interrupt them?"

"No, I daren't—she's protecting me. She knows, somehow, though I've never told her. And he seems to know she knows."

"Oh." Margaret felt despairing. It was so unlike Jonathan not to have a plan. Well, at least *she* could try.

"Find some of Uncle Peter's old clothes," she whispered, "ones he never uses. Take them down to the witch. Lucy's washing him. I'll do something to stop Mr. Gordon."

"Thank you," said Jonathan, and slipped off down the passage toward Aunt Anne's room. Margaret, her gullet hard with fright, crept back into Jonathan's room, out along the shed roof and down the ivy. It would have to be a lie—a good big one.

When she threw open the kitchen door Mr. Gordon was still rocking and clucking, and now Aunt Anne was leaning forward in her chair like a mouse which has caught the eye of an adder. Neither of them looked around when the door banged against the dresser, though she'd pushed it so hard that the blue cups rattled on their saucers.

"Oh, Aunt Anne, Aunt Anne," she croaked (and her

terror was real), "a ginger cat just spoke to me. He said 'Good morning.' "

The rocker stopped its clack. Aunt Anne eased herself back in her chair, gazed at the palm of her left hand, and then turned her head.

"What did you say, darling?" she said dully.

"I went down the lane to see if any of the crab apples had fallen at the back of Mrs. Gryde's, so that we could make some conserve, but before I got there a big ginger cat came out of the hedge from the six-acre and looked at me and said 'Good morning.' "

Mr. Gordon jumped out of the chair, sending his blackthorn stick clattering across the floor. Margaret ran to pick it up for him, but as she knelt his bony hand clawed into her shoulder, so that she dropped the stick again and almost shouted with surprise and hurt. He pulled her close to him; she could see the individual hairs that sprouted from the big wart on the side of his nose. His bloodshot old eyes glittered.

"Mrs. Gryde's cat, that'd be?" he said fiercely.

"No," croaked Margaret. "Hers is quite a little one. This was big, the biggest I've seen, and lame in one leg. It went away up toward the New Wood. Shall I show you?"

Mr. Gordon clucked once or twice, thinking. "Ah," he said at last. "That's where we found the witch. Mebbe he didn't go back to his master after all. Mebbe he turned hisself into a cat—and he'd be lame all right, after the stoning we give him. You bring me along and show me what you seen, lass."

He let go of her shoulder, but gripped it again the instant she'd turned. Aunt Anne had to scrabble for his stick. Then Margaret led him hobbling out into the road, hoping there were no witnesses about; but Mother Fatchet was driving her black pig up the slope toward them. Mr. Gordon stopped her, and the two old people at once began an excited cackling discussion about what might have happened, during which Margaret's invented cat seemed to grow bigger and bigger until she was afraid they wouldn't believe her when she showed them the rabbit run she'd decided on for it to have appeared through—a gravelly place where even the heaviest cat's paw-marks couldn't be expected to show up. But when she showed them the hole they didn't seem to mind that it was small. Mr. Gordon made her tell her lie all over again while he stared hotly up to where the young beeches of New Wood stood russet in the silvery sunlight. Then, at last, he let go of her shoulder and began hobbling up toward the center of the village to roust his cronies out of the pub for another witch-hunt. Mother Fatchet tied her pig to the farm gate and scuttled up the lane so that she should miss none of the blood-soaked fun.

Aunt Anne was at her stove, stirring uselessly at the big gruel pot which simmered there night and day. Margaret slid into the larder, opened one of the little bottles of cordial, poured half of it into a mug and placed that on the stove by Aunt Anne's left hand. Her aunt stopped stirring, picked up the mug and sniffed at it, looked sideways at Margaret, hesitated, then shut her

eyes and took three hefty swallows. When she put the
mug down she gave a long sigh and reached out to draw
Margaret close against her side, as though she was
afraid to say thank you out loud, as though even the
crannies and shelves of her own kitchen might be full of
spies waiting for the betraying word.

It would be dangerous to go back to the barn, Margaret thought—they wouldn't find anything up at the New
Wood and then they'd come to look for her to hear her
story again. When Aunt Anne let go of her she chose a
couple of bruised apples from the larder and ran out to
the paddock to talk to Scrub. He was sulking, jealous
after three days' neglect, and wouldn't come when she
whistled. But Caesar, Jonathan's unloved and melan-
choly gray, came boredly over and Margaret gave him
one of the apples and started to fondle his ears. This
was too much for Scrub and he cantered over with a
clownish look in his eye as though he'd only just realized she was there. She accepted his pretense and gave
him his apple too.

All at once she heard harsh voices shouting on the
other side of the road, up in the six-acre; she climbed
up onto the second bar of the gate and teetered there
trying to crane over the tall hedge. When that wasn't
any good she slid across onto Scrub's back and coaxed
him along toward the gap further down the field—difficult sitting sideways without saddle or reins, because
she had no control at all. But Scrub was in a mood to
show how clever he could be, and did what she wanted.

There were eight or nine men standing in a circle just

below the New Wood. Three old women in black watched them from twenty yards away. The men all had sticks or cudgels and were taking it in turn to beat something that lay on the grass in the middle of the circle; they shouted at each blow, egging each other on. She could recognize Mr. Gordon by his stoop, and Mr. Syon the smith by his apron, and the two black-bearded brothers from Clapper's Farm. While she was wondering sickly what they'd caught, one of the men struck so hard that he snapped his cudgel; he threw the pieces angrily on the ground and began to walk down across the six-acre toward her. As he came nearer she saw it was one of the stonecutters from the quarry on the Beacon: nearer still, and his cheeks were burning with cider though it was still only the middle of the morning.

"Think your uncle would mind if you lent us a spade, lass?" he shouted.

"I'll get one," Margaret shouted back. She slid off Scrub's back, climbed the fence and ran around to the farmyard. The stonecutter was already staggering in through the gate when she came out of the shed where the garden tools were kept. Aunt Anne had come to the kitchen door to watch.

"What did you find?" asked Margaret as she handed the big man the spade. Her fear and disgust must have sounded just like excitement to him.

"Ah," he answered with gloating pleasure, "he were a clever one, but he weren't so clever as he thought he were. He'd changed hisself into a rook, you see, so's to be able to fly away from where Davey Gordon could smell him out, but he'd forgot as how his arm was broke. The cat you saw was lame, weren't he, missy? So now he was a rook, his wing was broke, and he couldn't fly away after all."

The man gave a bellowing, cider-smelling laugh.

"We smashed him up, that we did," he shouted. "He won't do no more witching now. Thankee, missy—I'll fetch your spade back in half an hour. You done a good morning's work, you have."

He stumped out, too drunk to notice how white Margaret had turned, or how she reeled and hugged the well-pump to keep herself from falling. When the whole hillside and valley had stopped slopping around she found Aunt Anne standing anxious beside her.

"You'd best be away for a few hours, Marge," she said. "If I gave you a pot of damson cheese you could ride over to Cousin Mary's in the Vale. I should have sent it weeks back, but it slipped my mind. I'll pack you up a bit of bread and bacon, too, for your dinner. Mr. Gordon's sure to come round talking to Uncle Peter then, so you'd much best be somewhere else."

"Oh, thank you, Aunt Anne. I'll get Scrub ready."

Twenty minutes later Margaret was clear of the village, riding sidesaddle as she always did. She'd waved to old Mr. Sampson digging his cabbage patch by the almshouses; she'd craned over the Dower House wall to see the yew trees all clipped into shapes of animals; she had sniffed the thymy air as they came out of the woods, and leaned right down over Scrub's mane as the pony took the steep bank up the common grazing ground

below the Beacon; it was just like any of a hundred
other rides, hill and valley exactly the same as they'd
always been, as though nothing had happened to
change her world four days ago.

Scrub was skittish and restless with lack of exercise,
tossing his head sideways and up as though he wanted
to get a better grip of the bit; so she let him canter all
the way up the steady slope to the corner of the cemetery, where no one had been buried since the Changes
came because people preferred to be buried in the
churchyard even if it meant jostling the bones of long-
dead generations. As they swept around the corner they
hurtled into the middle of a swirling and squawking
white riot—they'd gone full tilt into the flock of village
geese. Scrub reared and skittered sideways with an awkward bouncy motion, but Margaret had had half a second to see what was going to happen, so she gripped
the pommel of her saddle tightly, allowed him a few
moments to be stupid (he knew all about geese, really)
and then reined him firmly in.

The geese subsided into angry gossip. Mother Fatchet's eldest grandchild was supposed to be herding them
but he'd taken time off to swing on a low branch of one
of the cemetery pines; now he jumped down, picked up
his long stick, put his thumb in his mouth and stood
watching her sulkily. Margaret said good morning to
him as she rode on, but he didn't answer. For the first
time she realized how suspicious everybody was nowadays—suspicious of strangers, suspicious of neighbors.
Anyone could betray you. Perhaps other villages were

different—friendly and easy—but this village was like a bitch with a hurt foot: move and it snarled.

Of course, people didn't *have* to like each other. Even sweet Aunt Anne had quarreled with jolly Cousin Mary, quarreled twenty years ago about a silver teapot. Now they never visited, never spoke; Cousin Mary sent Aunt Anne a pot of honey in high summer and Aunt Anne sent Cousin Mary a pot of damson cheese in late autumn, and that was all.

But nobody liking or trusting *anybody*—it couldn't have been like that before the Changes.

She made poor Scrub scrabble up the loose-stoned path to the very ridge of the Beacon, though it was just as short and much easier to go around the side. Another curious thing struck her: the great earth ramparts of the Beacon had been built thousands of years ago, before the Romans came, but she only knew that—only knew about the Romans coming, too—because she'd been told it before the Changes, when she was less than nine. Nobody told you that sort of thing nowadays: there wasn't any history. Everyone talked and behaved as though England had always been the same as it was now, and always would be; the only thing to mark one year off from another was a rick catching fire, or a bad harvest, or a big tree falling, or a witch being caught and stoned. No one ever mentioned the Changes, if they could help it.

And that was how she'd thought herself until four days ago, until Jonathan had spattered the petrol over the stocks and she'd remembered that seaside filling station.

She reined Scrub in for a breather at the very top of the Beacon, where the old triangulation point had been (some fanatic had managed to knock the cement into fragments with a sledgehammer), and looked at the enormous landscape with new eyes. Always before it had been the dim hills of Wales which had excited her, and the many-elmed green leagues between the two escarpments, and the glistening twists of the Severn. Now it was the gray smudge in the middle, Gloucester, the dead city.

Always before she had looked away from it, as though it were something horrible, a stone and slate disease. Now she wanted to see what it was like since all the people had left it. You couldn't live in a big city now: there was nothing to live on, no one to buy from or sell to; besides, the whole place must smell of the wickedness of machines.

Brookthorpe is the first village in the Vale, just as Edge is the last village in the hills. Margaret seldom rode down into the Vale, but she found a way by lanes and footpaths, cutting across fields where no path led in the right direction. There was much less arable land since tractors were gone, and cows were mostly herded by children, so many of the hedges had been allowed to go into gaps.

Cousin Mary had moved. A pretty young woman was living in her cottage and the old apple tree had been cut down. The new owner said that Cousin Mary had gone to live with a friend at Hempsted, right down by the river. She told Margaret how to get there.

The Vale has a quite different feel to it from the hills. It's not just that the fields are flatter and most of the houses are brick: the air smells different, and the people have a different look, sly and knowing; the farms are dirtier, too, and the lanes twist for no good reason (up in the hills they twist to take a slope the best way, or so as not to lose height when one is following a contour). Margaret had to ask her way several times, and the answer always came in a strange, soft voice with a sideways look.

She skirted a dead housing development, came to a rotary and rode north along a big road for nearly a mile, looking for a lane to the left. The buildings by the road were rusting old factories and garages, and sometimes a little group of shops with their windows broken and all their goods stolen. Cars and trucks rusted in forecourts, and pale tatters of advertising posters dangled from walls. One place, an open-air used-car mart, had been set on fire, for all the cars were twisted and charred; you'd only have to walk along the lines of them, taking off the filler-caps and poking blazing rags in with a stick —dangerous, but some people were fanatical against machines.

As soon as she'd turned off along the lane to Hempsted, Margaret had a disappointment. A bridge took her over a river, which she at first thought must be the Severn, only it seemed too mean and narrow. She stopped on the bridge and gazed north and south, and saw that the river ran unnaturally straight, and that there were man-made embankments on both sides and a path running all along its bank. So it wasn't a mean and narrow river but a man-made thing, a noble great canal, far wider than the silted thin affair that ran through Stroud. This wasn't dug for narrow barges, but for proper ships; she could see from the color of the water, a flinty gray, that it was deep enough to take seagoing vessels.

Supposing that they could get under the bridge. But no, that wouldn't be necessary, because the whole bridge was made to swivel sideways, out of the way of passing ships. There was even a crankhandle to turn it with.

She was still wondering whether the bridge would really have swung if she'd had the nerve to turn the handle, when she came into Hempsted. Cousin Mary's new house was a little cottage close in under the churchyard wall. Cousin Mary herself was busy forking dung into the tiny garden, but she stopped her work to receive the precious pot of damson cheese and to ask formally after all her relations up in the hills. She seemed to be not really "living with a friend" as the woman in Brookthorpe had suggested, but to be more of a servant here, like Lucy was on the farm. But she offered to take Margaret into the cottage and show her the place where she'd spilled boiling water on her leg, and it wouldn't heal because Mrs. Barnes down the road had put a spite on her. Margaret said, "No, thank you." There was a great tattered bandage around

Cousin Mary's leg, all yellow with new dung and older
dirt—no wonder it wouldn't heal. She said good-bye,
rode back to the little lane through Hempsted and
turned left. She was going to see what Gloucester
looked like.

There were houses all along the lane, with fields behind them. Their windows were broken and their tiles
were all awry. In a gap between two such houses a man
was digging; he stood up and shouted to her as she
passed but she couldn't catch what he said—it sounded
like something about dogs—so she just waved cheerfully to him. From the slight rise on which Hempsted
stands she could see the tower of the cathedral, and the
lane led straight toward it. She felt gay, almost heroic,
with her adventure, so it took her longer than it usually
would have to sense that Scrub was becoming more and
more uneasy. Only when he shied across the lane at a
big chestnut leaf that floated down in front of his nose
did Margaret pay attention to his feelings, and by then
they were on the edge of the city itself.

A level crossing over a light railway seemed to mark
the real boundary, and there she almost turned back.
She was hungry, and Scrub clearly was against going
on. But it seemed cowardly, having come so far. What
would Jonathan have thought of her? So she dismounted and led Scrub across the rails. The nape of her
neck began to prickle; the long, low buildings on either
side of the lane were windowless and very silent; by the
side of the railway she spotted a bar of rusty iron as
thick as a man's thumb and two feet long. She picked it

up before she remounted—any weapon was better than none.

The echo of Scrub's hooves tocked back at her off blank walls. In one place the surface of the road had heaved up where frost had reached a pocket of underground water, a burst main, perhaps. On the other side the road became a bridge.

It was a bridge over a canal, the same canal as they'd crossed earlier. On her left was a series of V-shaped gates, two facing inward to hold the water of the canal in, and one outward to control the fast-flowing river which swept round the long curve beyond. On her right were the docks, a wide basin of water surrounded by grim, tall warehouses, and cranes and derricks. Sunken barges lay along the quays, all green with weed. There were two proper ships, with masts and funnels, further down the basin, but one of them was leaning sideways in the water. And against the left-hand quay was a line of three smaller boats, two floating, one waterlogged; the floating ones sat oddly in the water, but looked as though that was how they were meant to be, stern down, bows up, stubby and pugnacious; their funnels were far too big for them. Margaret remembered a jig-saw which she'd been given once when she was ill, a picture of the *Queen Elizabeth* docking. There'd been boats like this in it. They were tugs.

Despite the peeling paint and the rust and the streaks of gulls' droppings they looked undaunted and power-ful, an example of the forgotten forces which were on the children's side, if they could be summoned into use again. Margaret began to feel cheerful once more.

But not Scrub. As they rode on, occasionally catching a glimpse of the cathedral tower to guide them, he was tense and quivering. Margaret talked to him to keep his spirits up, but then the sound of her own voice seemed so naked in the empty street that she let it dribble into a whisper, and then into silence. She patted him half-heartedly on the neck and wished she hadn't come.

The street bent left, in the wrong direction, following the curve of the flowing water. This again couldn't be the true Severn—it was too narrow and controlled—but it must be part of it. Then the street jinked right, away from the water, and crossed a much wider road which led back toward the hills. Margaret turned right.

She almost missed the cathedral because it lay off to the left of this larger road down a narrow alley, but she saw the knobbly pinnacles out of the corner of her eye and wheeled Scrub around into the cathedral grounds. The grass was long and rank, which once had been shaved as close as a mower could be set; it didn't even seem to have been nibbled by rabbits. All the doors were locked fast, so she rode around the gray mass wondering what it was like now inside; she had a dim memory of heavy and shadowed arches, with candles and high, lacy singing; but that might have been some other church. She rode back into the main street and on down to a big crossroads. The sun was halfway down the sky now, and that meant that the proper direction must be . . .

But as she considered the position of the shadows a white mongrel terrier ran out of a lane to her left, threw back its head and howled. The howl was answered by others from all around, and at once the terrier, very lean and dirty but very quick, sprang snarling toward her. Three more dogs wheeled out, baying, further down the left-hand road. Scrub shied, but she kept her seat and shouted and shook the reins. At once he was off up the street in front, the terrier yelping at his heels. Margaret glanced over her shoulder and saw that another dozen dogs poured out of side alleys and were tearing down the road after her. Scrub was already moving at a full gallop, jarring and frightening on the hard uneven road; there was no point in trying to make him go any faster—if he panicked they'd both fall at some pothole. She looked over her shoulder again. Now there were at least thirty dogs in the pack, trailing out all down the street, with the short-legged descendants of corgis and basset hounds far behind while the long-legged Labrador mongrels yelped at Scrub's heels.

A big, wolfish creature with a lot of Alsatian in him made a spurt and leaped, jaws wide, for Scrub's flank. But Margaret happened to be balanced just right to whang him across the forehead with her iron bar. She heard a bone crack and saw him tumble head over heels, and then her eye was caught by an interruption in the level of the road ahead. There had been some sort of explosion—gas perhaps—and fifty yards further on the whole width of the tarmac had been thrown up into a rough barrier which would slow a horse to a walk while the dogs came streaming over it. The streets on either side ran off at right angles, far too sharp to turn a galloping pony into. As they neared the upheaval she saw that right against the left-hand wall, up on the pavement, there was a gap. Scrub had been galloping down the middle of the road, between the blank traffic signals and unreadable police notices, but she coaxed him over toward the wall. He took the curb cleverly, flashed through the gap, pecked as his off forefoot banged into a loose brick, but recovered.

Only a rangy black Labrador was still with them now. Scrub could gallop faster than the dogs could run, but he couldn't keep it up for as long as they could—at least not with a girl and the heavy sidesaddle to carry as well. He would have to ease his pace soon. The black dog bounded along, just out of reach; Margaret lashed at it twice with her bar, but missed; the second time she so nearly unbalanced herself from the saddle that she had to let the weapon drop. Desperately she unbuckled her saddlebag, felt for a slice of bacon, held it out as one holds a chocolate for a begging lapdog, then tossed it in front of the beast's jaws. It slashed at the morsel and missed, but the smell of meat was enough to make it slide to a stop, turn and investigate. The rest of the pack engulfed it while it was still swallowing, then came on. Margaret dug into the saddlebag and flung piece after piece of her picnic behind her, until the street was filled with squabbling hounds. Only the slowest ones came too late to share the feast, and they followed halfheartedly on her trail. Soon she was a hundred yards ahead of the nearest one. Next time she looked around they'd all given up.

Scrub took some slowing, though. The road curved through a section of the city where all the houses had caught fire; it ran under a railway bridge and straightened again before he could be induced to canter, and then to trot. They were still going a fair lick when they came out into open fields and the road tilted toward the hills.

Two miles further on, among inhabited cottages once more, she dismounted and led him. His coat was rough and bristling, his cheeks and neck rimed with drying foam. Every now and then he tensed and gave a great heaving shudder. When the hill really began to slope steeply, beyond the turning for Upton, she led him onto a wide piece of grassy verge to graze and rest; there were two crusts of bread and a strip of bacon fat left for her lunch, and now it was nearly teatime, but she ate them thankfully, thinking that there are worse things than hunger. Then she looked over his hooves, though it was too soon to see how bruised he'd been by the punishing gallop along the tarmac.

They went home very slowly, Margaret walking most of the way. It was dark before they started down through the long wood that screened the village from the north, and she was already far later than even Aunt Anne's merciful errand would give her an excuse for; so just before she turned the lane where the farm lay she picked up a small stone and rammed it into the groove between Scrub's near front shoe and the tenderer flesh. She led him into the farmyard convincingly lame.

But all the playacting she'd prepared, all the believable lies, all the excuses—they were unnecessary. Uncle Peter was cock-a-hoop at the best milk yield of the year; Aunt Anne wanted to know all about Cousin Mary's new house; Jonathan talked busily about the fox cubs in Low Wood; Lucy was her usual secret self. Any stranger coming in would have thought them a nice, dull, contented family enjoying a plain supper after an ordinary day.

Chapter 3

THERE'S WICKEDNESS ABOUT

Margaret was full of sleep—as full as a ripe Victoria plum is of juice—but something was shaking her. Her dream turned it into a bear, and she was too heavy to run away, and she was opening her mouth to cry out for help when she was all at once awake. Not very awake; longing for the warm and private world of sleep again; but awake enough to know that it was Jonathan who was shaking her and the world was too dangerous to cry for help in. She tried to say "Go away" but the noise she made was a guggling grunt, a noise such as a bear might make while shaking a person.

"Oh, wake up, Marge," whispered Jonathan impatiently.

"I'm asleep. Go away."

"Never mind that. He wants to talk to us."

"Who does? The witch?"

"His name's Otto."

"Oh, all right."

She rolled on her back and with a strong spasm of willpower forced herself to sit up while the frosty night sent fingers of gooseflesh down her shoulder blades. Jonathan, thinking ahead as usual, had gathered her clothes onto the table below the window, where she could just see by starlight which way around she was picking them up; but she didn't feel warm even when she was dressed, and stood shivering.

"Shall I go down and get you a coat?" he whispered.

"No," said Margaret, remembering all the betraying creaks in the passage and on the stairs. "I'll be all right. I suppose we're going out through your window. What time is it?"

"Nearly midnight. I took some thistles to bed to keep me awake. Put your cushions under your blankets to make it look as if you're still in bed—Mother might look in—she often goes creeping round the house in the middle of the night. That'll do."

Outside, the frost was deep and hard, the true chill of winter. The stars were thick and steady between the apple branches, the grass crisp under her feet; dead leaves which had been soggy that morning crackled when she trod on them; the air was peppery in her nostrils. It would be hunting weather tomorrow.

As they stepped into the heavy blackness of Tim's shed Jonathan caught her by the arm and stopped her.

"He's ill," he whispered, "and Lucy says she thinks he's getting worse. I've put a splint on his arm and I tried to strap up his ribs, but I don't know if it's any use. He can't move his legs at all. Perhaps he'll die, and all we'll have to do is bury him. But if he's too ill to think and then he doesn't die, we've got to know what we're all going to do. We'd have settled it this morning without you, but Lucy said he was too tired after his washing; he took one of the last of his pills, which are for when something hurts too much, and they make him sleep for twelve hours. So he should be awake now."

She couldn't see at all, but let him guide her through the torn gap in the bare wall, between the bruising tractors and into the engine hut. Here there was a gentle gleam from the shrouded lantern, as faint as the light from the embers of a fire after the lamps are put out.

Lucy was asleep on a pile of straw in the corner, but twitched herself wide awake the moment they came in. Tim was already awake, bubbling quietly, watching them, sitting so close to the lantern that his shadow covered all the far wall. The witch—Otto—was awake too, his eyes quick amid the bruised face. His wounds looked even worse now that the blood and dirt had been washed away, because you could see how much he was really hurt.

"Welcome to Cell One of the British Resistance Movement," he said in his croaking voice. "I'm Otto."

"I'm Margaret."

"Pleased to meet you. I got a fever coming on, and we

should get things kind of sorted before. I could have tried earlier, but I figured you were some kind of trap. But Jo tells me I owe you my life, young lady. Such as it is."

"It was Jonathan really," said Margaret. "I wouldn't have known what to do."

"Well, thanks all the same. You reckon they'll stone me all over again if they find me?"

"Yes," said Jonathan.

"And what'll they do to you?" said Otto.

Margaret and Jonathan glanced at each other, and then across at Lucy. She shook her head slightly, meaning that they mustn't tell him, but his eyes were sharp and his mind quick with the coming fever. He understood their glances, plain as speaking.

"Kill you too?" he whispered. "Kids? What kind of folk are they, for God's sake?"

"Not everywhere," said Margaret quickly. "I mean I don't think it's the same all over England. I was wondering about that this morning. This village has gone specially sour, don't you think, Jo?"

"I don't know. I hope so, for the other villages' sake."

"They're so bored," said Margaret. "They haven't anything to do except get drunk and be cruel."

"It's more than that," said Jonathan slowly. "They've done so many awful things that they've *got* to believe they were right. The more they hurt and kill, the more they're proving to themselves they've been doing God's will all along. What do you think, Lucy?"

"That's just about it," said the soft voice from the corner.

"And what started it all?" said Otto.

"The Changes," said Margaret and Jonathan together.

"Huh?"

"We aren't allowed to talk about them," said Margaret. "But everyone woke up feeling different. Everyone started hating machines. A lot of people went away, and the rest of us have gone back and back in time, until . . ."

"But why?" said Otto.

"I don't think anybody knows," said Jonathan.

The girls shook their heads. Tim bubbled. The witch was silent for half a minute.

"Let's try a different tack," he said. "You three don't think machines are wicked. Nor my friend Tim, neither."

"Tim never did," said Lucy.

"I did until four days ago," said Margaret. "But I hadn't thought about them for ages. And I still don't *like* them."

"I do," said Jonathan. "It happened in that very hot week we had during haymaking; I was lugging water out to the ponies and I suddenly felt, Why can't we use the standpipe tap again?"

"Me too," said Lucy, "only it was the stove. I was cleaning it, and I remembered electric cookers didn't need cleaning—not every day, leastways."

"But everyone's afraid to say," said Jonathan.

"It's only worn off some people," said Margaret. "All the men still seem to believe it."

"Course they do," whispered Lucy fiercely. "It means everyone's got to do just what they says."

"It might be something to do with children's minds," said Jonathan in a detached voice. "Not being so set in their ways of thinking."

"Let it go," said the witch restlessly. "You'd best just cart me someplace else and leave me to fend for myself."

The three children were silent, staring at him.

"We can't," said Jonathan at last.

"Why not? You got me here."

"What about Tim?" said Jonathan.

"I don't think he'd let us," said Margaret.

"That he wouldn't," said Lucy.

They all looked to where Tim, scrawny and powerful, crouched amid the tousled straw. There was another long silence.

"Besides," said Jonathan, almost in a whisper, "d'you think you'd ever sleep easy again afterward, Marge?"

She shook her head. There was stretching silence again.

"Where do you come from?" said Jonathan at last.

"America. The States."

They looked at him blankly.

"Davy Crockett," he said. "Cowboys. Injuns. Batman."

Forgotten images stirred.

"Why did you come?" said Margaret. "You must have known it was dangerous."

"They wanted to know what was happening in these parts," said the witch. "I'm a spy. I had a little radio, and I was in the woods up yonder reporting back to my command ship when your folk burst in on me."

"Mr. Gordon smelled your wireless," said Jonathan. "He's like that with machines. You mean that this hasn't happened to the whole world? Only England?"

"England, Scotland, Wales," said the witch. "Not Ireland. Well, then, if Tim won't let you dump me somewhere, how are you going to keep me here?"

"I bring food for Tim," said Lucy. "I can bring enough for you, easy as easy. You won't be eating much, from the look of you."

"I don't like it," he muttered, more to himself than to them.

"We'll work out a story," said Margaret, "something they'll want to believe and that fits in with what they know."

She told them about the cat and the rook.

"And I do have a broken arm," muttered the witch when she'd finished. He was looking much iller now.

"Please, miss," said Lucy, "he's had enough of talking for now."

"All right," said Margaret, "we'll go."

She stood up, but Jonathan stayed where he was.

"What're we going to do if we think it's becoming too risky to keep him here?" he said. "We must have a plan."

"Yes," muttered the witch, "a plan. A man can plan. Can a man plan? Dan can plan, Anne. Nan can fan a pan, man. Dan . . . Dan . . ."

"He doesn't know what he's saying," said Lucy. "My dad went that way, sometimes, but it was drink did it to him. We shouldn't have kept him talking so long. I'm worried for him, I am."

"We'll have to think of something without him," said Jonathan. "Are you going to stay here all night, Lucy?"

"Aye," she said.

"But will you be all right?" said Margaret fussily. "It doesn't look very comfortable."

Lucy looked at her slyly out of the corner of her eyes. "I've slept worse," she said. "And it's one less bed to make, isn't it, miss?"

Outside the night air was cold as frozen iron. The moon was up now, putting out half the stars and making the shadows of the orchard trees crisscross the path, so black and hard that you lifted your feet for fear of stumbling over them.

"Jo," said Margaret, "I . . ."

He caught her elbow in an urgent grip; he seemed to know just where she was in spite of the dark. He put his mouth so close to her ear that she could feel the warm droplets condensing in her hair, like a cow's breath.

"Not out here," he whispered. "Sounds are funny at night. Inside."

She went up the ivy first, letting him push her feet into toeholds to save the noise of scrabbling among the hard leaves. She was shivering as she crawled along the wall and in through the window; by the time she was sitting on the edge of his bed, cold was all she could think about. Jonathan came into the room as quietly as a hunting owl, shut the window, opened his big chest (no creak—he must have oiled the hinges) and brought out a couple of thick furs. They wrapped the softness around themselves, hair side inside, and sat together on the rim of the mattress, as close as roosting hens, trying to feel warm by recalling what warmth had once been like.

"What were you going to say, Marge?" he whispered.

"I went right into Gloucester today. A pack of wild dogs chased me, but that wasn't it. Jo, there are real boats in the town; there's a sort of harbor in the middle of it, with a big canal full of water. If we could get him into one of those and make it go, we might be able to get him away."

"Sailing boats?"

"No, tugs. They sit a funny way in the water as if they were made for pulling things. Do you remember, we used to have a jigsaw puzzle?"

"I had a toy tug. I used to play with it in my bath, but the water always got into the batteries."

"Will these have batteries?"

"Don't be stupid. They'll have proper engines, diesel I should think. If there's a harbor, there should be big tanks with diesel oil in them; perhaps Otto will know how to make it go—he's an engineer, he told us while we were washing him. Lucy's marvelous: she doesn't seem to mind anything."

"One of them's sunk, Jo, but the other two look all right."

"It's been five years, Marge. Engines get rusty, specially sitting down in the water like that. I don't know if you could take a canal boat out to sea—you'd have to be very lucky with the weather."

"But it wasn't that sort of canal, Jo. It was big— twenty yards across, and there were proper ships there, sea ships."

"Oh. Where did the canal lead, then? Out into the Severn?"

"I don't know, but not where I saw, about two miles out of Gloucester. Why do you think it's still full of water? It's much higher than the river."

"They probably built it so that streams keep it filled up. The river wiggles all over the place and goes up and down with the tide and it's full of sandbanks too, I expect. It'd be useful to have a straight canal going out to sea, which you could rely on to have the same amount of water in it always. There'd have to be a lock at the ends, of course."

"What's a lock?"

"Two gates to keep the water from running away when a canal goes downhill or out to sea. You can make the water between them go up and down so that you can get a barge through."

"There were two gates—three gates—at one end, but I don't see how they'd work."

"I've explained it badly. I'll draw you a picture tomorrow. But even if the tugs don't actually go they might be a good place to hide the witch in."

"Provided the dogs don't swim out. They were horrible, Jo."

"Poor Marge. I'll ask him what he thinks tomorrow. Bed now."

But next morning, while Margaret was ladling porridge into the bowls Lucy held for her, the girls' eyes met. Lucy gave a tiny shake of the head, a tiny turndown of the corners of the mouth, before she moved away; so Margaret knew that the witch must be worse. It was a funny feeling, being part of a plot, sharing perilous secrets with somebody you never really thought of as a proper person, only a rather useless and lazy servant. But it was exciting too, especially being able to speak a language they both understood but which Uncle Peter and Aunt Anne didn't even see or hear being spoken.

After breakfast she helped Lucy clear and wash up and then make all the beds, a job she especially hated. Uncle Peter had hired a man to clear the undergrowth in Low Wood and tie all the salable sticks into bundles of bean poles and switches; this meant that he had to go and work alongside the man, partly from pride and partly to be certain he got every last groat of his money's worth out of him. And that meant that poor Jo had to muck out the milking shed after the first milking and take the fourteen cows down to pasture, and then do all the farmyard jobs which Uncle Peter would usually have done. It was midmorning before any of them was free.

They couldn't all slink down to the barn, and Margaret was the least likely to be missed.

The witch was very ill, she could see at once; flushed and tossing, his eyes shut and his breath very fast and shallow. The splint on his arm was still tight in its place, but she didn't like to think about his ribs as he fidgeted his shoulders from side to side. Tim knelt at his good elbow, gazing into his face and bubbling very quietly; when the witch's feverish thrashings threw the blankets aside Tim waited for the first faint beginning of a shiver and then drew them back over him as gently as snow falling on pasture. The moment the gray lips moved, Tim was holding a little beaker to them and carefully tipping a few drops into the dry cranny. There was nothing Margaret could do which Tim couldn't do better, so she sat down with her back against the engine, taking care to arrange a piece of sack behind her so that the rusty iron shouldn't leave its betraying orange streaks down her shoulders.

The witch fidgeted and muttered. Tim babied him, eased water into the tense mouth, bubbled and cooed. When Margaret had been watching for nearly half an hour in the dim light and was just deciding to leave, the witch sighed suddenly and deeply and the tenseness went out of his body. His head lay back on the straw, with his mouth open in a sloping O, like a chicken with the gapes. But this time Tim didn't pour any water into it; instead he watched for several minutes, at first with intense concern but gradually relaxing. At last he turned to Margaret, bubbled briefly and shambled out. She was in charge now.

Nothing happened in the first twenty minutes of her watch. The witch slept unmoving. The harsh lines of action relaxed into weakness until she could see how young he really was. Twenty? Twenty-one? She wondered how many times this had all happened before— the soldier, hunted and wounded, hopeless, lying feverish on dirty straw in some secret place while the yellow lamp burned slowly away. Hundreds of times, after hundreds of battles. But *this* time . . .

Then the lamp burned blue for a second, recovered, reeked with black fumes and went out.

Margaret sat in the dark, not knowing what to do. She could go up to the house and refill the lamp, or just get a new one; but it would be a funny thing to be seen doing in midmorning. And it would mean leaving him alone. And if she stumbled and made a noise in the dark she might wake him and sleep was better than medicine, Aunt Anne always said. She stayed where she was; it was quiet and warm and dark, and after the panics of yesterday and the busyness of the night she was as tired as a babe at dusk.

Voices woke her. Her legs were numb and creaking with the pain of long stillness, but she dursn't move because one of the voices was Mr. Gordon's.

"I smell summat," he grumbled.

"Smell, Davey?" said Uncle Peter's voice.

"Arrgh, not smelling with my nose—in my heart I smell it. There's wickedness about, Peter."

"Ah, 'tis nobbut those old engines in the big barn. There's a whole herd of 'em in there, Davey, but they're dead, dead."

"Mebbe you're right," said Mr. Gordon after a pause. "Mebbe you're not. That zany of yourn, Peter, what do you reckon to him?"

"Tim?" said Uncle Peter. Margaret could hear the lilt of surprise in his voice. "He's not in his right wits, but he's as strong as an ox."

"Mebbe, mebbe," said Mr. Gordon. "He'll bear watching, Peter. They're proper cunning, witches are. I wouldn't put it past 'em."

"Making out to be a zany, you mean," said Uncle Peter, still surprised. "But Tim's been with us these four years, and *I've* seen no sign of it. And why, Davey, I told you about the milk, didn't I—how much Maisie gave after we stoned t'other witch up in the stocks? But if Tim was one . . ."

"Your missus don't reckon 'twas more than a change of pasture as made the cattle give so well," said Mr. Gordon sharply.

"Don't you listen to what Anne says," said Uncle Peter with a growl. Mr. Gordon began to cluck. Very slowly, with a rustling like a cow browsing through long grass, they moved away up the orchard. It was minutes before she dared to shift a leg and endure the agonies of pins and needles. Just as the witch was stirring again there came the sound of someone moving quietly through the main barn; the door of the hut rasped as the rusty hinges moved.

"Why are you in the dark?" said Jonathan's voice, very low.

"The lamp went out," whispered Margaret.

"There's another one," he said. "You should have lit it from the old one before it went out. I'll run up to the house and fetch a new light."

"I'm sorry. I didn't know. Be careful, Jo—Mr. Gordon's been nosing round outside."

"Yes, I saw him. They've gone up to the pub, the Seven Stars. I won't be long."

The witch looked no better when the light came, despite his little sleep. Margaret tried to dribble a sip of water between his parted lips as she'd seen Tim doing, but made a mess of the job and spilled half of it down the stubble on his chin. Then she told Jonathan what she'd heard.

"We'll shift Otto as soon as we can, down to those tugs of yours in Gloucester Docks," said Jonathan. "No one goes there, and it's halfway home for him. If only we can last out till the snow comes we can take him down on the logging sledge."

"That'll be at least a month."

"I know. Will you tell Lucy or shall I? About Tim?"

"Tim?"

"What you told me Mr. Gordon said. They like the feel of killing now, that lot—smashing up rooks won't keep them happy for long. They want a real person, human, but somebody who doesn't matter to anyone."

"Except Lucy," said Margaret.

"They wouldn't think she counted. And even if Otto

wasn't here, if he was really dead, they'd come and search and find Tim's treasures and stone him for that."

"Jo, oughtn't you to come and see the tugs?"

"Father'll want me on the farm too much."

"Couldn't you sprain an arm or something—something that didn't stop you riding?"

"I suppose so. I ought to have a look at that canal too. I want to know how it gets out into the sea."

"Well, we've got a month," said Margaret. "We'll just have to be careful. I'll go and tell Lucy. Do you think Tim understands about being secret?"

"Sure of it—he's more like a wild animal than a person in some ways. I've noticed he never comes straight down here nowadays."

"How wrong in his mind do you think he really is, Jo?"

"What do you mean?"

"If he were in a country with proper doctors, like there used to be when we were small, do you think they could make him all right?"

"I don't know. Perhaps. We'll ask Otto when he gets better."

They sat in the yellow gloom for several minutes. All the bright outside world seemed more dangerous than this secret cave with the sick man in it; but when Tim came back they got up wordlessly and left.

Margaret found Lucy putting away a big basket of late-picked apples on the racks in the apple loft. She did it very badly, not looking to see whether any of them were bruised, and sometimes even shoving them so roughly into place that they were sure to get new bruises. Margaret started to tell her off, checked herself in mid-nag and said, "I'm sorry. Let me do it."

Lucy stepped away from the basket with her secret smile and Margaret's irritation bubbled inside her like milk coming up to boil over. With a wrench of will she stopped herself saying anything and began to stack the apples on the slats, gentling them into place so that none of them touched each other but no space was wasted. It was a soothing job; after she'd done the first row she told Lucy what she'd overheard Mr. Gordon saying about Tim. She finished her story just when the basket was empty, so she turned it over and sat on it. Lucy settled opposite, onto an old crate, biting away at a hangnail.

"Aye," she said at last, "that's just about Mus' Gordon's way. What did Master Jonathan say?"

"He said I was to tell you."

"He didn't have a plan, then, miss?"

"He thought we should try and move the witch down to Gloucester—I saw some boats in the harbor where he could hide—as soon as the first snows come and we can use the sledge. Perhaps Tim could go with him."

"That'll be a month, maybe."

"Yes, at least."

"But will the old men stay happy till then, without another creature to smash up, miss?"

"I don't know. I think we might be able to invent one or two things to keep them busy."

"Maybe."

"Lucy . . ."

"Yes, miss."

"I was talking to Jonathan about Tim. If he had proper doctors, like there were before the Changes, do you think they would be able to put him right in his mind?"

"That's why they took him away, miss. They put him in a special school, they called it. They said it was probably too late, but it was worth trying. Then, when the Changes come, my mum and dad took the babies to France—there were two of 'em, a boy and a girl. They wanted to take me, too, but the Changes were a lovely reason for not having to bother with Tim no more, so they was going to leave him behind. It wasn't right, I thought, so I run away and found him and took him away. Sick with worry they teachers was, half of them gone and no electrics no more and no food coming and a herd of idiot boys to care for—they was glad to see the back of one of 'em. So we traveled about a bit and then we come up here."

"I've often wondered," said Margaret. "Thank you for telling me."

"Yes, miss."

"But if we managed to get the witch away to America, you wouldn't mind Tim going with him?"

Lucy started on another nail, one that looked as if it had had as much chewing as it could stand.

"No telling, miss. He's happy here, now. *If* doctors could put him right in his mind, I'd like that. But if they can't, what then? A great big prison of a house, full of other zanies, that's most likely. He's someone here, miss, part of a family, even if he does sleep on straw. And now he's got Otto to fend for . . ."

"Oh dear," said Margaret. "But Mr. Gordon's got his eye on him for his next stoning."

"Aye," said Lucy. "But if it were only that I'd just take him away. We'd find another farm where they can use a maidservant and a strong lad. But it's no use talking of it—I couldn't part him from Otto now. It'd break his heart."

"Poor Tim."

"Don't you go fretting for him, miss. You fret for your auntie."

"I know," said Margaret. "Lucy, if you hear anything . . . anything *dangerous*, you'll let Jonathan or me know quickly, won't you?"

"Yes, miss."

She stood up, carelessly dusting her bottom, and slipped down the ladder. Margaret dropped the empty basket for her to catch and then followed.

The witch lay on his straw, too ill to make plans with, for four whole weeks. Sometimes he could talk sense, but very feebly. Twice they thought he was really better now; four or five times they thought he was dying. It was a hideous age of waiting.

But at least they didn't have to invent diversions for Mr. Gordon and his cronies, because two great excitements came to the village unasked. The first was a visit from the lord of the manor, a great earl who lived far up to the north, beyond Tewkesbury, but who had a habit of rushing around his domains attended by a great crowd of chaplains and clerks and falconers and ken-nelmen and grooms and leeches and verderers and landless gentlemen who had no job except to hang around, swell their master's retinue, and hope to be of service. Two of these clattered into the village three days after the midnight conference and rummaged around the houses looking for rooms where the small army could sleep. The squire had to move out of his house into the Dower House to make room for the great earl. It was like ripples in a pond all through the village, everyone being jostled into discomfort either to make space for one of the newcomers or for a villager whose bed had been commandeered. So Lucy had to make herself a bed on the floor of her little attic so that Margaret could sleep in *her* bed, so that Margaret's room could be occupied by a gentleman-groom, who slept in Margaret's bed, and a stableboy who slept on the floor. The stableboy normally would have slept in a room above the stables where his precious horses were housed, but the stables at the farm were really the cow-shed, and had no room above them. Space had to be cleared to milk the cows in the hay barn.

Lucy slept down in the witch's hut, in fact, but she had to have a bed in the house in case questions were asked.

The gentleman-groom was a shy boy, and the stable-boy was a garrulous old man. The gentleman-groom had to be up at the squire's house before dawn and didn't get back till after supper, but the stableboy had little to do except groom and exercise the rangy great horses and tell his endless stories. Margaret found herself spending all day in the stables, leaning against a silky flank and smelling its leathery sweat, while the stableboy talked about horses long dead, about the winners of the Cheltenham Gold Cup thirty years before (all the great earl's retinue rode what once had been steeplechasers or hunters). Sometimes his stories went further back, right into misty legends. He talked about Charles the Second staking the worth of half a county at Newmarket, about Dick Turpin's gallop to York, about Richard the Hunchback yelling for a fresh horse at Bosworth Field.

It didn't have to be racing: anything to do with the noble animals whose service had shaped his life was worth telling. One morning he sat on an upturned bucket and told her about the endurance of horses, about chargers which had fallen dead rather than ease from the gallop their masters had asked of them.

"I'm sure Scrub wouldn't do that," said Margaret.

"Neither he would," said the stableboy, "but he's a pony. Ponies ain't merely small horses—they're a different breed. More sense, they got. If ever you need to cross forty mile in a hurry, missie, you take a horse. But four hundred mile, and you'll be better off with a pony. They'll go an' they'll go, but when they're beat they'll stop."

"But there must be lots with mixed blood," said Margaret.

"Aye," he said, "but there's blood and there's blood.

Now I'll tell you summat. In the Armada, fifteen hundred eighty-eight, they Spaniards came to conquer England with a mortal great army, only they had to come in ships seeing the Lord has set us on an island, and Sir Francis Drake he harried 'em and worried 'em until they sheered off and ran right round the north of Scotland and back to Spain thataway. Only the Lord sent fearsome storms that year, and half of 'em sank, and one of the ships as sank had a parcel of Arab horses on her, and one of them horses broke free as the ship went down, and he swam and he swam through the hollerin' waves till he come to a rocky beach where he dragged hisself ashore, and that was Cornwall. And to this day, missie, the wild ponies in Cornwall have a streak of Arab in them plain to see."

"I didn't know horses could swim like that," said Margaret.

The stableboy ran a mottled hand along roan ribs, caressing the faintly shivering hide.

"It's the buoyancy," he said. "They got these mortal great lungs in 'em for galloping, so they float high. Swim with a grown man astride 'em, they will, always provide he leans well forward and don't let hisself slip off over the withers—they keeps their shoulders up and let their hinder end tilt down, y'see. If ever you want to swim with a horse, you hold on to the tail of it, or the saddle."

"But the waves," said Margaret.

"They holds their head that high the waves don't bother 'em," said the stableboy. "Mark you, they gets

frighted if they're not used to it, but I'd sooner be a
horse nor a man in a rough sea. We haven't the buoyancy, nor the balance neither. Too much in the leg, we
got, and only two legs at that. Now another thing,
missie . . ."

And he was off again on his endless catalogues of the
ways in which the horse excelled all other species, including Man.

Margaret was sorry when he left, swept off in the
storm of the great earl's progress. But at least Mr.
Gordon and his cronies had been kept active and interested for eight days and would have enough to talk
about over their cider mugs for a week besides.

The other excitement didn't happen in the village at
all. Just when the witch-hunters were tired of gossip
over the great earl's visit and were beginning to sniff the
wintry air for new sport, a messenger came over from
Stonehouse to say that two children had seen a bear in
the woods. Nobody had ever been on a bear-hunt, but
all the men seemed to know exactly what to do. Wicked
short spears were improvised and ground to deadly
sharpness; Mr. Lyon the smith forged several pounds of
extra heavy arrowheads, to penetrate a tough hide at
short range; the best dogs were chosen and starved.
Then all the men moved out in a great troop to hunt the
bear.

Mr. Gordon insisted on going too, maintaining that
the bear must be a witch who had changed his shape but
couldn't change back till the new moon, or had simply
forgotten the spell. Even his drinking companions pri-

vately thought it more likely to be a survivor from the
old Bristol zoo, but they didn't care to say so. Instead
they built a litter and took turns to carry it; he rode at
the head of the mob, hunched in his swaying chair,
cackling to his bearers.

The whole of the village changed when they had left.
Tensions eased; Aunt Anne smiled sometimes and began to look a little pink; the bursts of gossip you could
hear up the street were on a different note—the pitch of
women's voices; and it was quieter, so that between-
whiles the only noise was the knock of the hired man's
billhook cutting into an elder stump down in Low
Wood.

With Uncle Peter gone, Jonathan was busy all day on
the farm, but Margaret stole a satchel of food next
evening and asked Lucy to creep up and wake her an
hour before dawn. The stars were still sharp in the sky
when she set off to explore the canal, and Scrub's
breath made crisp little cloudlets in the frosty air. The
stars were sharp in the sky again when she got back to
find Aunt Anne waiting with a lantern in the porch.
Margaret reckoned she'd done over forty miles. After
supper Aunt Anne went out to visit a sick neighbor, so
the children pulled their chairs up around the red embers of the fire; but in a minute Lucy slid off hers and sat
right in under the chimneypiece, her cheeks scarlet with
the close heat and every little spurt of flame sending
elvish shadows across her face. Jonathan sat out in the
gloom, quite silent but twitching like a dreaming
hound. Margaret told them what she had found.

"I didn't start from the docks, Jo, because we can ride along that bit when we're taking food down to Lucy— besides, I didn't know how far I'd have to go the other way along the canal. It's miles and miles, and just the same all the way—just the canal and the path beside it. Except that at first it runs between banks and you can't see anything on either side, and later it's up above the rest of the country. *It* doesn't go up and down, of course, only the fields around it do. The towpath is easy to ride on, except for one bad stretch a little way down. There are lots of bridges—I counted them on the way back but I lost count—it's about fifteen, and some of them are open already. . . ."

"Open?" said Jonathan.

"Yes. It's like this: half the bridge is made of stone which juts out into the canal and doesn't move, but the other half's iron, all in one piece, and there's a big handle—you have to unlock the bridge at each end first with a piece of iron which you flip over—and when you turn the handle the whole iron part of the bridge swings around, very slowly though, until it's right out of the way and you can get a boat through. It's a funny feeling —you're moving tons and tons of iron, but it's all so balanced that it moves quite easily. There's a little cottage by each bridge where the people used to live who opened the bridges for the boats, but they're all empty now. Otherwise there aren't a lot of houses by the canal, except for a little village near the end. I got chased by a bull before that."

"Rather you than me," whispered Lucy. Jonathan laughed.

"It wasn't funny," said Margaret, "it was horrid. There's a place where you come out of woods and the canal goes for two miles straight as a plank, but the river's suddenly quite close, across the fields on the right. There's a bridge in the middle of the straight piece—it's called Splatt Bridge, it says; all the bridges have their names on them—and when I got there I thought I'd ride off across the fields and look at the river. I've never seen it close, and I was tired of the canal. The fields were all flat and empty, and I wasn't bothering when I came around a broken piece of hedge quite close to the canal, and it was there, black, bigger than any of the bulls in the village, not making any noise, rushing at us. Scrub saw it before I did, and he got us away, but only just. It was tethered on a long rope through a ring on its nose. It looked mad as Mr. Gordon, Jo, furious, it wanted to kill us, and it came so fast, like a . . . like a . . ."

"Train," said Jonathan. Margaret shook her head.

"I still can't think like that," she said. "I didn't like opening that bridge, Jo. Not because somebody might catch me, but just for what it was."

"Poor Marge," said Jonathan cheerfully. "Still, you got away from the bull. What happened then?"

"Then there's a strange bit, with the river getting nearer and nearer until there's only a thin strip of land between it and the canal; and everything's flat and bleak and full of gulls and the air smells salty and Wales is

only just over on the other side, low red cliffs with trees
on them. It's funny being able to see so far when you're
right down in the bottom like that, and the river gets
wider and wider all the time—it's really the sea, I suppose. And then you get to a place where you're riding
between sheds, and there are old railway lines, and
huge piles of old timber, some of it in the open and
some of it under roofs, and one enormous tower without any windows, much bigger than the tower of the
cathedral, and a place like the docks at Gloucester but
with a big ship—a really big one, I couldn't believe it.
And then you come to another lock; at least I think it's a
lock but it's far bigger than the Gloucester one and the
gates are made of steel or iron. And beyond that the
water's much lower, inside an enormous pool with sloping sides and places for tying ships to, and another gate
at the far end, and beyond that there are two enormous
wooden arms curving out into the river, and it's as wild
as the end of the world."

"How deep is the canal?" said Jonathan.

"About twelve feet. I measured it with a pole I found,
from two of the bridges. And I couldn't see anywhere
where it looked reedy and silted. There's a place about
halfway along where a stream runs into it, which could
help keep it full. How does a lock work?"

Jonathan took a twig and scratched in the film of gray
ashes which covered the hearthstone.

"It's like this," he said. "The water in the canal is
higher than the water in the pool, so it pushes the top
gates shut. If you want to get a boat out, you push the

bottom gates shut, and then you open special sluices to let the water in the canal run into the lock. The new water holds the bottom gates shut, and the water in the lock rises until it's the same level as the water in the canal and you can open the top gates. You sail into the lock and shut them again, and then you shut the top sluices and open the bottom ones and the water runs out of the lock until it's the same level as the water in the pool, and you can open the bottom gates."

Lucy came around and stared at the scrawled lines.

"I don't know how they think of such things," she said at last.

"I see," said Margaret. "At least I sort of see. Oh, Jo, can't we find a big sailing boat and not try to make any beastly engines go?"

"No," said Jonathan. "It would have to be a very big one to go to sea in winter, and all the sailing boats which are big enough will have men on them, using them and looking after them. Besides, we'd never be strong enough to manage the sails, even with Tim's help, and we wouldn't know how, either. But if Otto can show us how to start one of the tugs, then we've got a real chance."

Chapter 4

FIRST SNOW

The men came back on the third day, arguing among themselves all the way up the winding hill. Nine villages, it seemed, had gathered for the hunt, and all their eager sportsmen had so hallooed and trampled through the flaming beech groves that the dogs had never had a chance to smell anything except man-sweat. Mr. Lyon had broken an ankle, though; and several small animals had been slaughtered, including five foxes; and Mr. Gordon and his cronies had spent the whole of the second day digging out a badgers' set and killing the snarling inmates as they uncovered them. Mr. Gordon's litter still swayed high above the procession as they tramped wearily up by the churchyard, and in his hand he waved a stick with the gaping head of a badger spiked on its end.

They were busy with boasting for several days after that, and then with critical discussions of the behavior of the people from other villages. So it was thirty-six days (Margaret reckoned them up) after Mr. Gordon had last come nosing around the farm before he came again.

This time he arrived while she was helping Aunt Anne with the heavy irons, lifting them off the stove when you could smell the burning fibers of the cloth you handled them with and carrying them back when they were too cool to press the creases out of the pillow-case. It was a peaceful, repetitive job until the latch lifted and the hunched shape stood outlined against the sharp winter sunlight.

"Mornin'," he grunted, and without waiting for an invitation hobbled across and settled himself in Uncle Peter's chair.

"Good morning, Mr. Gordon," said Aunt Anne, and started to iron a shirt she had just finished with an iron which was already cool. Mr. Gordon clucked.

"Sharpish weather we're having," she said after a while. "There'll be snow before the week's out."

Mr. Gordon clucked again.

When Margaret brought the freshly heated iron she could sense how tense her aunt was. At first she'd hoped to slide away, but now she saw she would have to stay, just in case she could help.

"That Tim," said Mr. Gordon suddenly. "What d'ye reckon to him?"

"Tim?" said Aunt Anne, surprised. "He's just a poor zany."

"Aye," said Mr. Gordon slowly and derisively. "Nobbut a poor zany."

He sat and rocked and clucked while Aunt Anne carefully nosed her iron down the seam of a smock.

"Where'd he come from, then?" he shouted suddenly. "Answer me that!"

Aunt Anne jerked her body upright with shock, and dropped her iron. It made a slamming clatter on the flagged floor.

"I think he came from Bristol," said Margaret.

"Aye, Bristol," muttered Mr. Gordon. "Wicked places, cities."

"That's true," said Aunt Anne.

Mr. Gordon clucked and rocked.

"Why do you want to know?" said Aunt Anne in a shivering voice.

"There's wickedness about," said Mr. Gordon. "I can smell un. It draws me here, same as a ewe draws her lamb home to her."

There was no answer to that, so Aunt Anne went on with her ironing and Margaret with her fetching and carrying of the heavy irons. Mr. Gordon watched them with fierce little eyes amid the wrinkled face, as though every movement was a clue to the wickedness which lay hidden about the farm. The kitchen seemed to get darker. Margaret found she couldn't keep her mind off the witch, tossing feverish on dirty straw. She tried to think about Scrub, or Jonathan, or even Caesar, but all the time the picture inside her skull remained one of dim yellow lantern light, the rusty engine, Tim squatting patient in the shadows, and the sick man whose presence drew Mr. Gordon down to this peaceful farm.

Twice Aunt Anne started to say something, and twice she stopped herself. When Margaret took a new iron to her their eyes met: Aunt Anne's said "Help!" as plain as screaming.

Next time Margaret fetched a hot iron she went over toward the open hearth as if to chivvy the logs, tripped over the corner of the rug, and sprawling across the floor brought the rim of metal hard against the old man's shin. He cried out with a strange, high bellow, leaped to his feet, and before she could crawl out of reach started to belabor her over the shoulders. She cringed under two stinging blows before she glimpsed Aunt Anne's shoes rush past her face; then there was a brief gasping struggle. When she came trembling to her feet Mr. Gordon was slumped back in the chair, panting, and Aunt Anne was standing beside him, very flushed, holding his stick in her hand. They all stayed where they were for a long while, until the rage and panic had faded from their faces. At last Mr. Gordon put out his hand for his stick.

Aunt Anne gave it to him without a word and held the rocking chair steady while he worked himself upright. He took one step, gasped, felt for the arm of the chair and sat down.

"Ye've broken my leg, between ye," he said harshly. "Fetch your man, missus. I'll need carrying."

Aunt Anne walked quietly out into the farmyard, leaving Margaret and the old man together. She wasn't afraid of him for the moment; the fire seemed to have dimmed in his eyes. She began to be sorry she'd hit him so hard until he looked sideways at her from under his scurfy eyebrows and muttered, "No child was ever the worse for a bit o' beating."

Margaret slipped away to the foot of the stairs, where she waited until Uncle Peter came. As soon as he heard the heavy footsteps Mr. Gordon started moaning and groaning to himself. Margaret gritted her teeth and waited for another beating, but Uncle Peter paid no attention to her. Instead he stood in front of Mr. Gordon's chair with his hands on his hips and gazed down at the crumpled figure.

"What the devil d'ye think you're up to, Davey?" he said. "Laying into my kin without my leave?"

Mr. Gordon stopped groaning, gave a pitiful snivel and looked up at the big, angry man.

"I'm hurt, Pete," he said. "Hurt bad. Get me home, so as I can lay up for a couple of days."

"Let's have a look at ye," said Uncle Peter curtly. He knelt down and, pulling out his knife, ripped open the coarse leggings. There seemed to be no end of sackcloth before the blue and blotchy shank came into view. Margaret tiptoed forward and saw where there was a small red weal on the skin that stretched over the shinbone. Now she wished she'd hit him harder.

"I'll fetch the barrow," grunted Uncle Peter, "and I'll wheel you up to the Stars. Two jars of cider and ye'll be skipping about, Davey. But don't you take it into your head to wallop my kin again, not without my say-so.''

He lashed the leggings untidily back into position and went out. There came the rumble of an iron-shod wheel on the flagstones outside; then he strode into the kitchen, lifted Mr. Gordon clean out of the chair and carried him to the door. As he turned himself sideways to ease his burden through the gap Mr. Gordon gave a wild cackle.

"Ah," he cried, "what I couldn't do if I was as strong as yourself, Peter lad."

The words sounded forgiving, but the voice rang with mad threats. Uncle Peter didn't say anything, but carried him out and dumped him in the barrow and wheeled him up into the lane.

That afternoon, when she went out to tend to Scrub's needs and poor old Caesar's, she found the stonecutter from the quarry leaning on a low place in the hedge. She called a greeting to him, but he didn't say anything, only watched every move as she walked to and fro. She went back into the house when she'd finished and looked out of an upstairs window; he'd moved up onto the little knoll in the six-acre from which it was possible to see almost every movement on the whole of the farm. He stayed there until it was too dark to see.

Darkness, in fact, came early, under low heavy clouds; but in the last moments of daylight she saw a few big snowflakes floating past the window. There was an inch of chill whiteness in the yard when she went out to the cowshed to tell Uncle Peter it was time for supper. He

was milking the last cow, Daisy, his favorite, by the light
of a lantern set on the floor by his stool; the beams were
full of looming shadows, and she couldn't see his face
when he looked up.

"What the devil happened in the kitchen this morning, Marge?" he said. "Davey will have it you banged his
leg a-purpose."

She hesitated, taken by surprise, until it was too late
to lie.

"He was worrying Aunt Anne," she said. "I didn't
think she could stand it anymore, and I thought I had to
try and do something. It was the best thing I could do.
Do you think I was wrong, Uncle Peter?"

"No," he said slowly. "No. But Davey's not so crazed
as he acts. Just promise me one thing, Marge. You
haven't been mucking around with wicked machines,
have you, Marge?"

"No, really, I haven't. I promise." She was surprised
and frightened. If they didn't get the witch away soon,
they'd all be found out.

Uncle Peter turned slowly back to his milking, leaning his cheek against Daisy's haunch as though he were
listening for secrets inside her.

"All right," he said at last. "I believe you. But I won't
spare nor hide nor hair of you if I find you've deceived
me. That's a promise."

"Yes, Uncle Peter. But can't we do something to help
Aunt Anne? He doesn't seem to let her alone."

"I don't know, Marge. Honest I don't. Davey's a
weird one, but he wouldn't come worriting down here if

he didn't feel something was wrong. I don't know what
it is. Mebbe he's right about Tim."

"Oh, no!" cried Margaret. "Tim's only a poor zany.
He wouldn't hurt anyone."

"You never know," said her uncle darkly. As he stood
up and lifted the heavy bucket from under Daisy's bag
he said it again, almost to himself, as though he were
talking about something else: "You never know."

A glance and a warning jerk of the head were enough,
so tense were the children, to call a council after they
had all gone yawning up to bed. They sat in the dark in
Lucy's room, furthest away from where the adults slept,
and talked in whispers. It was very dark outside, with
snow still floating down steadily from the low cloud-
base. Margaret told them everything that Mr. Gordon
had said and done, and then what Uncle Peter had said
in the milking shed. When she'd finished she heard
Jonathan stirring, then saw his head and shoulders
black against the faint grayness of the window.

"If we went now," he said, "the snow would blot out
the marks of the runners."

"Now?" said both the girls together.

"Yes. And if we leave it for another night the snow
will be so thick that everyone will be able to see the
tracks going down to the barn, and we'd never be able
to get the sledge across the valley anyway."

"Oh dear," whispered Margaret. Her shoulders began to ache for a mattress and her neck for a pillow.

"Tim must come too," said Jonathan. "And you,
Lucy—you'd go with him if he ran away, wouldn't you?

They'll just think you overheard something that was being said and decided to take him away. You could stay if you really want to, Marge, but Scrub will pull much better if you're there. Besides, you know the way."

"I could tell you," said Margaret sulkily. "You go up Edge Lane and then . . . then . . . no, it's much too difficult. I'll have to come."

"Good," said Jonathan. "I don't think I could do it alone, honestly. Lucy, there's a pair of Father's boots drying in the pantry. We'll take them for Tim."

Lucy sighed in the dark. "I've never been a thief before," she said.

"You aren't now," said Jonathan. "I'm giving them to you."

Scrub didn't seem at all surprised to be harnessed and led through the orchard to where Jonathan had dragged the log-sledge. While Lucy and Jonathan cajoled Tim into his new boots, and then, talking very slowly, persuaded him to carry the witch outside into the dangerous night, Margaret picked up Scrub's hooves one by one and smeared them with lard from a little bowl which she had taken from the larder. That meant the snow wouldn't ball inside his shoes.

All the time the soft, feathery flakes of snow floated down. When they brushed her cheek they felt like the down from the inside of a split pillow, but when they rested for more than a second on bare flesh and began to melt they turned themselves into nasty little patches of killing cold. Tim came cooing out into the darkness. The witch groaned sharply as he was laid on the sledge, made comfortable, and then wrapped by Jonathan in an old tractor tarpaulin.

"Tim," whispered Lucy, "we're going. Going away. We're going."

Tim's bubbling changed, deepened, wavered and then restored itself to its usual note. He lurched into the darkness and they heard him scrabbling in the straw of his shed; then he came back and knelt by the sledge; the tarpaulin rasped twice as he readjusted it. Margaret realized he was taking his treasures with him.

It is steep all the way up to the ridge of Edge Lane. Margaret led the pony between the dark walls of silent houses, only able to see where the road was because of the faint glimmer from fallen snow. The runners of the sledge whimpered gently as they crushed the fluffy crystals to sliding ice. Tim's boots crunched and his throat bubbled. Once or twice Scrub's shoes chinked as they struck through the soft layer of whiteness to a stone underneath. Otherwise they all moved so quietly that Margaret could hear the tiny pattering and rustling of individual flakes falling into the dry leaves of Mrs. Godber's beech hedge.

Scrub took the slope well enough, but Margaret was beginning to worry how he'd manage the real steeps down into the valley and out again, where sometimes the lane tilts almost as sharply as the pitch of a roof. But at least she could see better now. As they came to the short piece of flat at the crest she understood why: the sky ahead really was lighter. Soon they would come out from under the snow cloud into starlight.

"I'll take the brake," said Jonathan. Margaret had been so rapt in her world of stealth and silence that she was startled to hear him speak aloud. She reached up to pat Scrub's neck and steady him for the descent, then heard the iron spike on the end of the brake bar beginning to bite through the snow into the pitted tarmac. Scrub plodded on, unamazed; but when a hundred yards down the hill and just as they were getting to the steepest place, the moon came out and he saw the treacherous white surface falling away at his feet, he snorted and tossed his head and tried to stop. The brake grated sharply as Jonathan hauled at it, but even so the sledge had enough momentum to push the pony forward onto the frightening decline. She felt the wild tide of panic beginning to rush through his blood, and put her hand right up inside the cheekstrap, so that she could at least hold his head still.

"Easy," she said. "Easy. Easy. You'll do it easy."

For a second she thought he wasn't going to believe her. Then he steadied and walked carefully down.

"That's the worst bit," said Jonathan.

The stream in the bottom was a black snake between the white pastures; it hissed like a snake too, and moonlight glistened off its wavelets as it might off polished scales. The old mill, which somebody had rebuilt just before the Changes, was a ruin again now; nobody cared to live so far from the village. They halted for a minute to allow Tim to move the witch around so that his feet would be below his head during the climb.

"We aren't going fast enough," said Jonathan. "It'll be morning before we get back."

"It's not so bad after Edge," said Margaret, "and it'll be much easier with the moon out."

She looked around at the black trees, the ruined mill, the white meadows with the black stream hissing between them; everything in the steep and secret valley looked magical under the chill moon. She'd never have dreamed that a world so dangerous could be so beautiful.

There are two very steep stretches on the far side. Jonathan showed Lucy how to work the brake, then cajoled Tim into hauling on one of the traces on one side of the sledge while he took the other. Scrub stumbled on the second slope, but was on his feet and pulling almost at once, which was lucky because Lucy was thinking about something else and hadn't even begun to use the brake. The pony's knees seemed unhurt, thanks to the cushioning snow, and he toiled bravely on.

Edge, on the last rim of the Cotswolds, was fast asleep, and the road to Gloucester curved through it and into the darkness of beechwoods.

"Do you think you could ride him down here, and get him to trot for a bit?" said Jonathan as soon as they were past the last inhabited house. "There's room for the rest of us on the sledge."

It meant rearranging the sick man again, but they crowded onto the rough slats, with Jonathan at the back to work the brake and Tim clutching the sack of food

Jonathan had stolen from the farm. Scrub was uneasy about the changed arrangement, and suspicious of the surface beneath his feet, but Margaret coaxed him into a trot. He faltered, changed pace to a walk and tossed his head.

"Oh, don't be silly," said Margaret. "It's quite safe, and you'll enjoy it. Come on."

She felt his mouth with the reins and nudged his ribs and he tried again, and this time he kept it up. The slope was just right for the sledge: left to itself it would have stopped, with that weight on it, but it needed very little pulling to keep it going and in a minute Scrub had completely changed his mind about the whole affair and was tugging at the bit and trying to stretch into a canter. Margaret looked over her shoulder to her passengers as they passed through a patch of moonlight where no trees masked the sky. Tim was crouched over his sack, staring out sideways at the blinks of light between the trunks. Lucy was smiling her elf smile, looking as wild as the wind that slipped icily past her. Jonathan perched on a nook of sledge between the witch's head and the brake bar, looking intently forward, ready for the next disaster. They could never have got this far without him: he knew what to do because he had thought about it before it happened—and he could think in secret because nobody could tell what was going on behind that funny crumpled face.

"Scrub wants to go faster," she shouted.

"Provided you don't miss your turn," he shouted back. "Throw your hand up when you see it coming."

The next few minutes were heroic adventure—real as the touch of timber but quite different, as different as dreams, from the everyday bothersomeness of roofs and clothing. The icy night air burned past her, long slopes of moonlit snow opened and closed on her left as the trees massed and thinned, Scrub covered the dangerous surface with a muscled and rhythmic confidence while she moved with his movement as a curlew moves with the northwest wind, and the road curved down the long hillside with the generous swoops imposed by the contours—and all the time a lower level of her mind kept telling her that what she was doing was dangerous. And right. Dangerous and right. Right and deadly.

Something nicked the corner of her awareness, the corner of her eye as they raced past—the cottage before the turn. She threw up her arm for a second (you could trust Jo to rely on the briefest signal) and busied herself with the problem of coaxing Scrub to a walk without letting him fall. The brake grated harshly just as she let him feel the pull of the bit.

"Too good to last, boy," she said.

He understood at once, slowing as fast as was safe on that surface and with the danger of the sledge banging into his hind legs. (No horse is really happy about pulling something which hasn't got shafts down a slope—he can't hold it back.)

The ten yards into the lane after the turn is very steep, as steep as Edge Lane, but they took it slowly. After that it levels out and they were able to trot several times, but the exhilaration of the ride down the main road was lost. The night was wheeling on; the high, untended hedges closed them in; they began to feel the secrecy and strangeness of the Vale; the empty city now seemed very near.

"Cheer up, Marge," said Jonathan while they were all rearranging themselves to allow Scrub to cope with a slight rise. "We've just about caught up with the time now. You tired?"

"Not if I don't think about it."

"Is there any way round Hempsted? Someone's bound to hear us with everything so quiet."

"I don't know. Anyway, I probably couldn't find it. This is much the best way in, because the houses are only just on both sides of the road, and not spread out in a great mass. If we try some other way we might meet the dogs."

"All right."

If anyone heard them in Hempsted they gave no sign. It was impossible to tell when they were out of the little inhabited village and into the derelict suburbs. Scrub was tiring now, difficult to coax out of his stolid walk. Margaret dismounted and walked beside him. Tim came and strode on the other side of him, as though he felt some mysterious sympathy with the weary limbs. The moon blanked out, and then there was a swirling flurry of snow, much more wind-driven in this open flatness than it had been up in the hills. Margaret bent her head and plodded on, looking only at the faint whiteness of the road a few feet in front of her. The

level crossing told her that they were nearly there—
otherwise she might have trudged on forever.

The snow shower stopped again just as they reached
the docks, but the moon didn't come out for several
minutes, during which she edged forward onto the quay
in a panic lest someone would fall into the bitter water.
Her memory was mistaken, too; there seemed to be far
more obstructions and kinks in the quayside than she'd
remembered in the quick glance from the bridge. Then
suddenly the light shone down between the blind warehouses and they could all see the whole basin.

"Those were the ones I meant, Jo," she said.

"Yes, the middle one's no good. It must be half full of
water. I'll nip ahead and nose around. You come on
slowly."

He flitted off between the shadows and was lost. Margaret heard a faint clunking. Scrub was worried and
restless, and she herself was too tense to calm him. The
water in the basin looked as black as polished slate.
Jonathan came back.

"I've found one which will do for the time being," he
said. "There's enough room for all three of them, and
we needn't try and get Otto down a ladder—I forced
the door of the wheelhouse. We can cast off one hawser
and slack off the other one and just shove her out into
the middle of the basin. Then there shouldn't be any
trouble from dogs. But I'm worried about water."

"Water?"

"For them to drink. The stuff in the basin doesn't
smell too good."

"Couldn't we melt some snow?"

"Good idea. You scout around and see if you can find something big enough to hold it. Tie Scrub up. Lucy, bring Tim along and I'll show you what I want."

Margaret explored all along the side of the quay, groping into shadows and waiting until the faint light reflected from the snow allowed her to distinguish the blacker shapes of solid objects amid the general blackness. She had in her mind's eye some sort of galvanized iron washtub, and didn't pause to wonder whether any such object was likely to be found in a commercial dockyard, so she came back to the tugs empty-handed after twenty minutes' search. The witch had vanished from the sledge and Tim was gone too. Jonathan and Lucy were performing a curious dance round a chimney-shaped thing, hopping, bending and half straightening before they hopped again. As Margaret came up Jonathan dragged the chimney thing a couple of yards further on.

"No luck, Marge?" he said. "Never mind. Lucy found an old oil drum with the lid off. I think it'll be all right—it holds water because we tried it in the dock, and it's not too dirty. Give us a hand."

So Margaret joined in the bending and hopping ritual, scooping up the light snow and throwing it into the drum.

"That'll do," said Jonathan at last. "We won't be able to carry it if it gets any heavier. Hang on, Lucy, while I make a lashing; we'll have to get it down into the hold or it won't melt. Fetch that bit of rope you found while I try and get my fingers warm enough to make knots."

Margaret suddenly felt the bitter numbness in her own fingers and put her hands under her armpits and jigged up and down in the puddled snow to get her blood moving. Jonathan swung his arms against his ribs with a dull slapping noise while Lucy slid off into the dark. When she returned there was a long period of just watching and feeling useless while Jonathan fiddled and fussed with the rope. Then Lucy fetched Tim and persuaded him to lift the drum onto the tug and lower it down a hatch.

"That's fine," said Jonathan. "There should be enough melted by morning to drink. Don't drink the water in the basin. Now we'll put you out to sea. All aboard. Got that pole, Lucy?"

"Yes, master," said the quiet voice.

"Show Tim how to push against the quay. I'll shove with my leg. Marge, hang on to my hand so that I can let myself go a bit further, otherwise I'll fall in. Off we go. All together now."

Margaret held his hand and prepared to lean backward against the weight of his stretch out over the water. Lucy found a good hold for the tip of her piece of timber; Jonathan began to shove; Lucy made Tim hold the pole where she'd been holding it and said, "Push. Push. That's right." Nothing happened for what seemed a long time, so that Margaret was sure that the basin must be silted up and the tug stuck. Then, suddenly, she saw a gleam of light between Jonathan's feet, and the oily blackness of the water around the ripple of reflected moonlight.

"Hang on, Marge," said Jonathan. "Don't let him fall over, Lucy. That's enough. We don't want to shove it right round the other way."

He hauled himself back onto the solid stone, and together they watched the tug drift, inch by inch, out over the water.

"That's fine," said Jonathan at last. "Lucy, you'll have to keep an eye open. If you find yourself drifting too near the quay again Tim can pole you off. And if you want to get ashore just haul on the hawser. You've got enough food for three days, I should think. Marge or I will be down again with more before Friday. All right?"

"Yes, master, and my thanks to you. And to you too, Miss Margaret." Her silky whisper drifted over the water. Far off in the city a dog bayed. Then the moon went out.

"We must be off," said Jonathan. "Do you think Scrub can stand it?"

"Yes. He's been eating snow, which is just as good as drinking, and I think he's found some grass in that corner. He's had a good rest, haven't you, boy?"

She knew he had heard the baying of the dog, and could feel the slight shivering of fright through his hide as she patted him in the pitch dark. He moved eagerly as she untied his reins from the stanchion, and she had a job walking as fast as he wanted to go along the treacherous cobbles, all littered with frozen hawser and rusting chains beneath the snow. Out on the road she climbed into the saddle and heard Jonathan settling at the back of the sledge. Scrub chose a quickish trot and bounced along the winding flat. They both got off to walk up the slight slope into Hempsted, but rode again down to the bridge over the canal.

"Marge," called Jonathan as they crossed the black water, "couldn't we have come along the towpath? It must be quicker."

"I expect so. I didn't think of it. Anyway, it was too dark to be safe."

"Let's try next time we come down."

"Yes."

Then there was the easy straight along the big road that leads to Bristol and another fair stretch along the winding lane toward hills which seemed darker and taller with every pace. In one brief patch of moonlight she saw that it hadn't snowed here since they came down, for the lines of the sledge's runners slashed clear through the soft whiteness and between them were the scuffled ovals of Scrub's hoofprints. Her legs were very tired when she dismounted to begin on the long climb up to Edge, and felt tireder still when the snow started again before they were halfway up to the main road. So there was nearly an hour's slow plodding (head bent, shoulders hunched, little runnels of melting coldness beginning to find their way into the cringing skin) before they could once again start down the hill to the valley. Margaret was too tired to think about risks; she let Scrub take it at a dangerous, wallowing canter through the dizzying flakes. Jonathan had to shout to warn her at the two very steep places, but she didn't even dismount then, only slowing the pony to a slithering walk while the brake scraped behind them. She had to walk up the far edge of the valley, and it took years of darkness (though she knew from daytime blackberrying that it was really only ten minutes' stroll). Then they were in the village again, coming down between houses with the snow falling as thick as flour from the runnel of a millstone. She could see neither sky nor star nor horizon through the swirling murk, but the habit of living without clocks told her there were two hours till dawn. She led Scrub into his paddock, heartlessly leaving him to lick snow and rummage for grass, while Jonathan dragged the sledge back into the timber-store.

When she came reeling back to the tack room with the harness and the heavy saddle he was waiting for her.

"Marge!" he hissed, as though he had something vital to tell her. "She's called *Heartsease.*"

"Who is?" said Margaret.

"The tug. I spelled it out by moonlight. It's the name of Mother's favorite flower—I thought it might be lucky."

"Luck's what we need," said Margaret crossly. She hung her gear in the darkest corner, shifted a dry saddle and reins to the place where she usually kept hers, and then, wet and miserable as a storm-wrecked bird, climbed the freezing ivy, crept along the passage, hid her wet clothes under the bed, snuggled between sheets and allowed herself to drown in sleep.

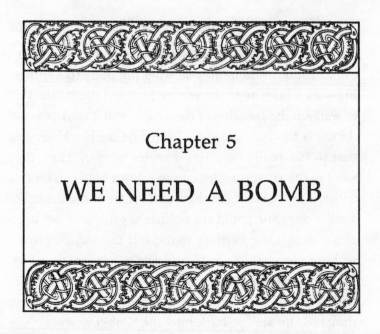

Chapter 5

WE NEED A BOMB

But even in sleep there was no safety. She dreamed about the bull which had chased her at Splatt Bridge, and woke from the nightmare in a wringing sweat, to lie in the faint grayness of first light and remember how huge and murderous he had seemed, how slowly Scrub had answered the rein and then had vanished, so that she was standing in the sopping grass while the bull hurtled down toward her, foaming, mad, untethered . . . It was a long time before she slept again.

The proper morning began with bellowings, not a bull's but Uncle Peter shouting and slamming around the house. Luckily this happened when the light was already broad across the uplands and the unmilked cows beginning to low plaintively in the shed, because (as often happens when the first snow falls) everyone slept longer than usual. Margaret dozed on, conscious at moments of the rummaging and thumping, until in the middle of a meaningless dream her shoulder was grasped and shaken hard. She opened her eyes and saw Aunt Anne, still in her nightrobe, face taut with worry, bending over the bed.

"Marge, Marge," she whispered.

Margaret sat up into the numbing air.

"What's the time?" she said.

"Marge, they've gone, Tim and Lucy, and they've taken Pete's second pair of boots and a shoulder of mutton and some bread. What shall I do?"

"Does he know what they've taken?" The habit of secrecy kept Margaret's voice low.

"No. I noticed the boots. He's mostly cross because the stove isn't lit and the porridge not on."

"I'll light it. Lucy must have heard Mr. Gordon talking to you. I shouldn't tell him anything. Can't you just be sleepy, Aunt Anne? If he's really angry he won't notice."

"He's milking the cows now. But what's happened to them? In this weather, too?"

"Oh, I'm sure they're all right. Lucy knows what she's doing."

Margaret realized as she spoke that she'd got her emphasis a little too strong. Aunt Anne stared at her, opening and shutting her mouth several times.

"What about Jo?" she hissed at last.

"Jo?" said Margaret, misjudging the surprise this time. "Has he gone too?"

Aunt Anne's bony fingers dug into her shoulders and she was shaken back and forward until her head banged the wall and she cried out aloud.

"You know what I mean," whispered Aunt Anne.

"Yes," said Margaret, "but you can't stop Jo doing what he wants to, can you?"

Aunt Anne sat on the bed and said, "No. No. Never."

"I'll do Lucy's work until you can find someone else. Can't you tell Uncle Peter it'll be two mouths less to feed through the winter? And you could tell him what Mr. Gordon said too—then he'd know why they've gone—I'm sure he's worried about it. I was talking to him in the cowshed last night."

Aunt Anne began to rock to and fro on the bed, moaning and saying, "Oh dear, oh dear." Margaret sat and waited for her to stop, but she went on and on until Margaret was frightened enough to slide out of bed and run along the passage to find Jonathan, who was yawning while he dressed.

"Come quick," she whispered. "Your mother's not well."

He walked to her room and stood for several seconds in the doorway, watching the rocking figure. Then he slipped his arm around her waist, pulled her wrist over his shoulder and walked her back toward her own bedroom.

"Get some breakfast for Father," he said as he went

through the door. "Don't dress—go down in your gown."

So there was kindling to be fetched from the scullery and the fire to be lit in the still-warm stove and little logs to be fed into it through the reeking smoke (that chimney was always a pig in a north wind) and the pots and kettles to be arranged in the hottest patches. Uncle Peter stormed in before anything was ready and threw himself into his chair where he glowered and growled. Margaret tiptoed to the larder and found a corner of boiled bacon and one of yesterday's loaves; while she was looking around for something to appease an angry and hungry farmer she noticed the little bottles of cordial, so she unscrewed the top of one and poured it into a pewter mug, which she carried into the kitchen and put on the table at his elbow. He picked it up, sniffed it and took a sip. When she came back with the bread and bacon he was tilting the mug to swallow the last drop. He banged the pewter back onto the table.

"Ah, that's something like," he said. "You've the right ideas, Marge girl."

"I'm afraid it will be twenty minutes before I can give you anything properly hot, Uncle Peter."

"Never mind, lass, never mind. I'll make do."

He picked up the thin, gray-bladed knife and hacked off a crooked slice of bread and a crookeder hunk of bacon.

"Gone!" he shouted through a mouth full of yellow teeth and munched crumbs and lean and fat.

"Aunt Anne told me," said Margaret.

"But why, but why?" shouted her uncle. "After all we did for 'em, too!"

"I think she must have overheard what Mr. Gordon was saying about Tim. Shall I fetch you another bottle of cordial?"

"Aye. No. Aye. No, better not. Bring me a mug of cider. What was Davey saying, then?"

"About Tim really being a witch. You were talking about it too, yesterday evening."

"Ah. He's a deep one, Davey. What do you think now, Marge, hey?"

"I don't know. I still don't see how a zany could be a witch. This porridge is warm enough to eat now— would you like some?"

"Leave it a minute more. I like it proper hot. You go and dress, lass, and I'll fend for myself. I must go and tell Davey Gordon what's up, and soon as may be."

Margaret spun out her dressing, and when she came down again the kitchen was empty. She opened the door into the yard and looked out; Uncle Peter's footmarks were the only blemish on the level snow, great splayed paces striding up toward the gate. If you knew what you were looking for you could just see two faint dimplings running side by side toward the shed—the lines made by the sledge runners when they'd come back, but covered with new-fallen snow; the marks of their outward journey had vanished. She turned at the sound of a light step behind her; Jonathan had sidled up to study the black-and-white landscape.

"Jo, I thought of something," she whispered. "Won't someone notice that the sledge is wet?"

"I left it under the hole in the roof, where there was piles of snow coming in. I put some bundles of pea-sticks over the place when we left, so the ground's fairly dry underneath too. It ought to look all right."

"How's Aunt Anne?"

"I don't know. Tell anyone who asks she's got a fever."

Then Mr. Gordon and his cronies came catcalling down the lane and trampled to and fro over the yard until even the marks of Uncle Peter's first crossing were scuffled out, let alone the lines left by the sledge. Mr. Gordon stood in the melee, head thrown back to sniff the bitter air.

"Clear!" he cried at last. "Sweet and clear! Peter, your farm's clear of wickedness now, or my name's not Davey Gordon."

"The zany, was it?" cried one of the stonecutters.

"Sure as sure," cackled Mr. Gordon. "And that sister of his, too, like enough."

"She always had a sly look," said another of the men. "Where'd they come from, anyone know?"

"Bristol," called Margaret from the porch.

"Aye, so you told me before," answered Mr. Gordon. "That's where they'll be heading then. Out and after them, boys."

But it was a quarter of an hour before the men even left the farm, because they kept telling each other how right they were, and repeating old arguments as if they

were new ones. Amid this manly furor no one spared a
second to ask after Aunt Anne; and when they departed
Uncle Peter went with them.

He left a hard day's work behind for two children
who'd been up most of the night—the cowshed to be
mucked out, hay carried in, ponies to be tended, sheep
to be seen to, hens to be fed and their eggs found, the
two old sows to be fed too—besides all the most-used
paths to be shoveled clear before the snow on them was
trodden down to ice too hard to shift. Jonathan ran
down to the stream and fetched the hired man to help
with the heaviest work, so by the time Uncle Peter came
back, bored with the useless hunt and angrily ashamed
with himself for leaving the farm when there was so
much to be done, most of the important jobs were
finished. Aunt Anne stayed abed all day, and Margaret
was staggering with tiredness when she carried the
stewpot to the table for supper; but she opened another
bottle of cordial for him (Aunt Anne rationed him to a
bottle on Sundays) and he leaned back in his chair and
belched and scowled at the roofbeams.

"Glad we didn't catch 'em, sort of," he said suddenly.

Margaret cleared away in a daze of exhaustion and
went to bed. When she looked down from the top of the
stairs he was still lolling there, his cheeks red in the
firelight and mottled with anger and drink, and his
shadow bouncing black across the far wall. He looked
like a cruel old god waiting for a sacrifice.

Too tired to bother with lanterns or candles she felt
her way into bed and dropped at once into that warm

black ocean of sleep which waits for bodies strained to the edge of bearing, and slept too deep for dreams.

Next day Aunt Anne seemed worse. She lay under her coverlet with her knees tucked almost up to her chin, and all she said when anyone tiptoed in to offer her a mug of gruel or a boiled egg was "Leave me alone. Leave me alone." Uncle Peter, after two attempts to comfort her (quite good attempts—worried, voice gentle), lost his temper with the unreasonableness of other folk and stumped off around the farm, furiously banging the milk pails together and when milking was done starting on the unnecessary job of restacking the timber pile and refusing to be helped. Margaret took him out a flagon of cider in midmorning (having poured half a bottle of cordial in first) but was otherwise far too busy with housework and cooking to pay attention to him or anyone else. Luckily Aunt Anne had done the baking two days ago, so there was bread enough for two days more, but even so there were hours of work to be done. When you have no machines, a household can only be kept sensible if certain jobs are done on certain days of the week, others on certain days of the month, others every day, and others fitted in according to season. Margaret usually hated housework; but now that Aunt Anne was moaning and rocking upstairs she was in charge, so she polished and scrubbed and swept with busy pleasure, humming old hymn tunes for hours on end.

It was only when she was laying the table for lunch that she realized that Jonathan was missing; she ran out to the paddock, and found that Caesar was missing too. Scrub trotted up for a gossip, but she could only spare him a few seconds before she ran back to clear the third place away, to pour the other half-bottle of cordial into Uncle Peter's tankard so that he wouldn't notice when she sploshed the cider in on top, and to think of a good lie. Luckily the stew smelled rich enough to tempt an angry, hungry man.

"Where's that Jo?" he said at once when he saw the two places.

She ladled out the best bits of meat she could find and added three dumplings (Aunt Anne would frown and purse her lips when she found how lavish Margaret had been with the precious suet).

"I sent him down to Cousin Mary," she said. "She's got a bad leg and I didn't know how she'd be making out this weather. I know Aunt Anne doesn't speak with her, but I thought she'd rather we did something than that we didn't."

Uncle Peter chewed at a big gobbet of meat until his mouth was empty enough for speech, if only just.

"We'd all be happier if we hadn't any relations," he growled. "None at all."

Margaret tried to sound shocked, because that was obviously what he wanted.

"What a horrid thing to say—why, you wouldn't have any of us!"

He laughed, pleasedly.

"Aye, maybe," he said, "but a man ought to be able to choose."

He scooped up another huge spoonful of stew, which gave Margaret time to think what she was going to say next.

"But then you wouldn't have anybody who *had* to stick by you. You'd only have friends and . . . and people like Mr. Gordon."

He munched slowly, thinking it his turn.

"Right you are," he said. "But mark you, I didn't choose him neither. He chose me. And what I say is . . ."

Between mouthfuls he told Margaret more about the village than he'd told her in years. Mr. Gordon was right, but he had too much power and influence for a man in his station, and that had maybe turned his head a trifle. It was squire's fault, and parson's. Squire was a ninny and parson was a drunkard. The whole village was sick. But you couldn't fight Davey Gordon and his gang, because nobody else would dare stand up for you. It was better to belong with them, and then at least you knew where you were. And, certainly, Davey had an uncanny nose for witchcraft of all kinds, and it was better to live in a sick village than one riddled with witches. And mark you, Marge girl, witch-hunting was good sport—better than cockfighting.

When he'd finished his harangue Margaret fetched him bread and cheese and went upstairs to see whether she could do anything for Aunt Anne. She was asleep at last, straightened out like a proper person. Margaret slipped out and settled down to a long afternoon of housewifery. She was feeding the eager hens in the early dusk when Jonathan came back, riding Caesar, who looked bewildered by the distance he'd suddenly been taken, as if he'd never realized that the world was so large.

"How's Mum?" said Jonathan in a low voice.

"Better, I think; anyway she's asleep and lying properly. I told your father you'd gone to see whether Cousin Mary was all right."

"Good idea. Our lot are, anyway. Lucy's found a little rowboat and tethered the tug right across the dock so that she can't drift about—she's a clever girl, given the chance. And she and Tim got Otto down into the cabin, where there's a stove, so they won't freeze. I took them enough food for three days, I hope."

"Did you try the footpath?"

"Yes, but there's a locked gate across it, so it was a good thing we didn't try it. It would be faster than going through Hempsted, if I can break the gate open. I didn't see your dogs, but I heard them; if they smell Lucy and the others it's going to be much more dangerous visiting the dock."

"But couldn't we tow them further along the canal, down to the bit beyond Hempsted? No one lives there or goes there."

"I can't start the engines, supposing they'll go, until Otto's well enough to show me how, and once they're started they'll bring people swarming round. When we do go, we'll have to get down the canal and out to sea all in one rush."

"If you can break that gate, Scrub could tow them for a few miles: that'd be enough."

"You and your Scrub! Could he really?"

"Oh, yes, I think so. You're so busy thinking about machines that you never remember what animals can do."

"Well, you think about them enough for both of us."

"Not so loud, Jo!"

"It's all right—it'd look funny if we spent all our time whispering to each other. Next time we can both get away I'll climb out the night before and hide that old horsecollar in the empty house at the top of Edge Lane. We mustn't be seen taking it."

But that wasn't for a full week. Aunt Anne's mindsickness left her, but a strange fever followed it which made all her joints ache whenever she moved, so she lay drear-faced in bed or else tried to get up and do her duty as a farmer's wife with such obvious pain that Margaret couldn't possibly leave her to cope. Twice Uncle Peter had to carry her up to her bed. Then he asked around the village for somebody to take Lucy's place and found a cousin of Mr. Gordon's who'd been living over in Slad Valley. Her name was Rosie, and she was a bustling, ginger-haired, sharp-voiced woman of thirty, chubby as a pig and with sharp piggy eyes which watched you all the time. Margaret and Jonathan agreed it was like having an enemy spy actually in the house, but at least her presence gave them the chance to get away for a whole day. Jonathan had been to the boat again, alone, in the meanwhile, but they both knew that the food on *Heartsease* must be getting low now.

They picked up the hidden horsecollar and rode down to the canal, Caesar still absurdly astonished at the amount of exercise he was suddenly expected to take after years of slouching about unwanted in the paddock. It had snowed several times since their mid-night journey, so the world was starched white except for the scribbled black lines of walls and hedges and the larger blobs where the copses stood; the colors of the famished hedgerow birds showed as sharp as they do in a painting. It had frozen most nights, too, and the sur-face of the snow was as crisp as cake icing but gave with a cracking noise when the hooves broke through to the softer stuff beneath. (This wasn't the cloying snow which would stick and cake inside the horseshoes, so there was no need to lard the ponies' feet.) The lane was hardly used this weather, but an old man waved at them from where he was chopping up the doors and staircase of an empty and isolated cottage to carry home for firewood.

"Seasonable weather we'll have for Christmas, then," he called.

"Yes," they shouted together.

"I'd forgotten about Christmas," muttered Margaret as they took the next slope. "It's going to make things much harder."

"Easier, I'd say," said Jonathan cheerfully. "With all those folk coming and going, no one will notice whether we're there or not."

"They'll notice if there's nothing to eat, so unless your mother gets better I'll have to be there."

"Won't Rosie . . ."

"If I leave her to do all the work she'll start asking people where on earth I can have got to—innocent, but meaning. You know."

"Um. Yes. We can't risk that, seeing whose cousin she is, too. And another thing, when we've shifted *Heartsease* we'd better go and call on Cousin Mary. Messages get sent at Christmas, and if we keep using her as an excuse and never go there, someone might hear tell of it."

"Besides," said Margaret, "she seemed terribly lonely when I did see her."

In front of the inn at Edge stood a group of men with short boar-spears in their hands, and rangy dogs rubbing against their legs. They waved, like the old man down the lane, but their minds were busy with the coming hunt and the ponies padded by as unnoticed as a small cloud. The runner-lines of a few sledges showed on the big road, but when they dipped into the lane the snow was untrodden—the Vale had little cause to visit the hills, nor the hills the Vale. As they twisted between the tall, ragged hedges Margaret glimpsed vistas of the flat reaches below, dim with snow, all white patches like a barely started watercolor. It looked very different from her earlier visits.

But when they were really down off the hills it felt just the same. As soon as the lane leveled out they came across a bent old woman gathering sticks out of the hedgerow. She glanced piercingly at them as they passed, but gave them no greeting. There was a black cat sitting on her shoulder. She looked like a proper witch.

She was the only soul they saw for the rest of the journey (not many, even of the queer Vale folk, cared to live so close to the city). When they crossed the swing bridge Jonathan reined Caesar to a willing halt and gazed up and down the mottled surface where the snow had fallen and frozen on the listless water. It looked a wicked surface, cold enough to kill and too weak to bear.

"I'm stupid," he said. "I should have known it would be like this. We can't tow her out till it thaws—for weeks, months, even."

"Wasn't it frozen when you came down on Tuesday?"

"There were bits of ice on it, but it was mostly water. I think the river must have risen high enough to flood over the top gates—that would have broken up the first lot of ice."

"What shall we do, then?"

"Go and see them, tell them to look out for the dogs, see how Otto is, give them the food. Then go and visit Cousin Mary."

The path by the canal was flat and easy, but long before they came to the dock area it was barred by a tall fence of corrugated iron. Jonathan led the way up the embankment, through a gap in a hedge and into the tangled garden of one of the deserted houses between Hempsted and Gloucester. Beyond the level crossing he pushed at a gate on the right of the road, picked his way between neat stacks of concrete drainage pipes and back to the canal. They were just below the docks.

"I found this way last time," he said. "There she is."

He pointed along the widening basin. The tug lay in its private ice floe right in the center of the dock, with a hawser dipping under the ice at prow and stern and a dinghy nestling against her quarter.

"It'll be easier from the other quay," said Jonathan. "We'll find a cord and throw it out so that they can pull the food sack across the ice—that hawser's shorter. Over this bridge is best."

"I can't see anyone on her," said Margaret.

"Too cold. They'll be keeping snug down below."

They moved in complete silence up the quayside and around an arm of frozen water which stretched south from the main dock until they reached the place where the hawser was tied—a chilly and narrow stretch of quay under a bleak cliff of warehouse. Margaret peered nervously into the cavernous blackness between its open doors, and then squinted upward to where, eighty feet above her, the hoisting hook still dangled from the black girder that jutted out above the topmost door.

"Ahoy!" called Jonathan.

He was answered by a clamor of baying from the other side of the dock. There was a swirl of movement along the far quay, a shapeless brown and orange and black and dun weltering which spilled over the edge and became the dog pack hurling across the ice toward them.

"In here!" shouted Jonathan, using the impetus of

Caesar's bucking to run him under the arch into the warehouse. Scrub followed, dragging Margaret.

"Door!" he shouted. She let go of the bridle and wrenched at her leaf of the big doors. It stuck, gave, rasped, and swung around into the arch. She could see the foremost dogs already on this side of the tug, coming in long bounds, heads thrown back and sideways, jaws gaping. Then Jonathan's door slammed against hers and they were in total dark.

"Sorry," he said, "mine was bolted."

He fiddled with the bottom of the doors while Margaret tensed her back against them and the baying and yapping rose in a spume of noise outside. The dark turned to grayness as her eyes learned to use the light from two grimed windows set high in the furthest wall. She could see the ponies now, standing quite still as though the dark were real night—just the way parrots go quiet when a cloth is thrown over their cage.

"I think that'll hold it," said Jonathan. "Hang on, there's a hook here too. That's better. Let's go up and see if we can see anything from above. If there isn't another way out we're in a mess."

The steps to the floor above were more of a broad ladder than a staircase. They found another long room, piled high with sacks of grain which had rotted and spilled their contents across the small railway that ran along the middle of the space from the doors overlooking the dock. The air smelled of mustiness and fermentation, sweet and bad.

"Let's go higher," said Jonathan. "They'll get excited

again if we open these doors, but they mayn't notice if we go right to the top."

Each floor had the same layout, with the double doors at the end and the railway down the middle between the stacked goods. Different kinds of goods had been stored at different levels; on the second floor the trolley that ran on the rails had been left half unloaded, with two crates of canned pineapples still on it and a ledger loose on the floor. The very top floor was used for the most miscellaneous items—there was even a bronze statue of a soldier in one corner, swathed in the ropes that had been used to handle the crates on the hoist; beside him lay several truck axles. The roof had gone in a couple of places and patches of snow lay on the floor, but this meant it was much lighter; and when Jonathan pulled the double doors open it felt like sunrise. The girder arm of the hoist stuck out rigid above them, the big hook dangling halfway along. It was a gulping drop to the quay below. Out on the ice the dog pack were sniffing round *Heartsease* in an absentminded but menacing way. Jonathan leaned against his side of the doorway, quite unaffected by the chilling drop, and teased the back of his skull.

"We need a bomb," he said.

"Oh, surely they wouldn't store them here," said Margaret. "The army would have . . . ."

He grinned across at her and she stopped talking.

"What's on that trolley?" he asked.

This one hadn't been unloaded at all. It was covered with small wooden boxes, no larger than shoeboxes, whose labels, still faintly legible, were addressed to the *Gloucester Echo.*

Margaret tried to pick one up but found she couldn't move it.

"Printing metal," said Jonathan. "Must be almost as heavy as lead. The boxes are small, so that a man can lift them. Now that's what I call a real bit of luck! Let's see if we can push it. Come on, harder! One, two, three, *heave!* Fine. Leave it there and we'll try the hoist. It'll be electric, but there might be a hand control to run the hook out. Tell me if anything moves."

He tugged levers without result, then began to turn a large wheel.

"That's it," said Margaret excitedly, but still without any idea of what he was up to.

"Good. Now those bits of iron at the end of the rails must be to stop the trolley flying out over that quay if there's an accident, but there might be a way of moving them."

"Mine's got a sort of hook this side."

"So's mine, hang on, it's stuck. Can you see anything to bang it with? Yes, that'll do. Ouch! Don't worry, I only grazed my knuckles. Done yours? Fine. Now, just let me work this out."

"But, Jo, even if you get them right under here, on the quay, you'll only hit one or two, and . . ."

Jonathan stopped sucking his ravaged knuckle to grin at her.

"I've got a better idea. If it works," he said.

He looked outside, up at the hoist, back at the trolley,

down at the drop. Then he wound the hook in, so that
he could reach it. Then he made Margaret help him
shove the trolley right to the giddy verge. Then he
fetched the ropes which festooned the bronze soldier
and spent several minutes contriving a lopsided sling
from the hook to the trolley. Last of all he wound the
hook out almost to the end of the girder and readjusted
the ropes. Margaret suddenly saw what would happen if
the trolley were pushed the last few inches over the
edge—pushed with a rush: it would swing down and
out, in a wide curve, trolley and boxes all moving together; but because the far end of the trolley was on
longer ropes than the near end, the boxes would start
to slide out forward, and when the swing of the ropes
had reached its limit the boxes would all shoot on and
be scattered right out across the ice, almost as far as
Heartsease; and if the dogs could be lured onto the ice at
the right moment . . . she knew what his next words
were going to be before he said them.

"You'll have to be bait, I'm afraid."

"Bait?"

"Yes, as soon as I've found a lever. I want them on the
ice halfway between here and *Heartsease*—it's the big
ones that are the killers. Go down to the bottom, edge
one door open, make quite sure you know how to shut
it, slip through and shout. Look, they're bored with the
tug and they're going back to where they were before,
so you'll know just how long it will take them to get
across. Stick it out as long as you can, Marge, but get
back inside when the first dog is halfway between the

boat and the quay—I don't want to drop a ton of lead on *you*. If I shout, you'll know it's not safe to open the door. All right?"

"All right," whispered Margaret, sick with terror. The stairs seemed longer going down, the rooms darker, the rustling of rats more obvious—perhaps they'd been scared into brief silence by the clamor of the dogs. Scrub and Caesar were restive: most ponies hate rats. She patted and talked to them both, until she realized she was only doing so to put off opening the door. She walked down between the rails and studied the bolt and the hook—the hook would be quite enough by itself. She was lifting it when she suddenly wondered whether she could hear him down all those stairs, supposing he was shouting to warn her of prowling hounds . . . come on, girl, of course you would— Jonathan wouldn't have suggested it if it wasn't going to work. She opened the door eight inches and slipped through the gap into the bitter daylight.

The dogs were over by a warehouse on the far side of the ice, squabbling over something edible. She could hear distant snarlings.

"Ahoy!" she called. Her voice was weak and thin.

"Ahoy!" came Jonathan's cheerful yell far above her head.

She saw two or three dogs raise their muzzles and look across the ice. She pranced about on the quay, waving both arms to make sure she was seen, because most dogs have poor vision and the wind was blowing from them to her, so that no scent would reach them.

At once it all became like the nightmares you have again and again: the same baying rose; the same swirl of color spilled down on the ice; the same dogs leaped yelping in front, their heads held the same way; the same panic lurched up inside her. She was yards from the door, after her prancing, and rushed madly for it, but when she reached it she saw that the dogs had barely come as far as the tug, so she still had to stand in the open, visible, edible, luring them on. Bait.

But it was only seconds before the first dog reached the rumple in the ice she'd chosen as a mark, and she could slip back in and hook the door shut. As she closed out the last of sky she thought she glimpsed black blobs hurling down.

Then there came a thud, a long, tearing crack, a lot of smaller bangings; the yelping changed its note, faltered and vanished; then there were only a few whimpers, mixed with a sucking and splashing. She unhooked the door, edged it open and poked her head out.

The whole surface of the ice had changed—it had been nothing like as thick as she'd thought and was really only snow frozen together, without the bonding strength of ice. Now the under water had flooded out across a great stretch of it and the part between her and *Heartsease* was smashed into separate floes, overlapping in places and leaving a long passage of open water. The smaller dogs had not come far enough to be caught and were rushing away to the far quay, but most of the larger ones were struggling in the deadly water. As she watched, one which had been marooned on a floating island of ice shifted its position; the ice tilted and slid it sideways into the water; it tried to scrabble back but could find no hold; then it swam across to the fixed ice and tried there, but still there was nothing on the slippery surface for its front legs to grip while it hauled its sodden hindquarters out; it tried and tried. Margaret looked away, and saw several others making the same hopeless effort around the edges of the open water. In the middle two still shapes floated—dogs which had actually been hit by the falling boxes. She shut the door and went trembling up the stairs.

Jonathan had shut his door and was sitting on a bale with his head between his hands. He looked white, even in the dimness.

"It worked," she said, "but I couldn't go on looking."

"Nor could I," he answered. "It's not their fault they're killers."

Margaret was surprised. She was so used, after five years of knowing him well, to his instant reaction to the needs of any happening that she hardly thought about it. Jo would say what to do, and he'd be right. Now, for the second time—the first had been when they'd crouched at the top of the stairs and listened to Mr. Gordon hypnotizing Aunt Anne—he'd buckled under the sudden load of his feelings. He felt the death of the dogs more than she did—she was only shocked, but he felt something deeper, more wounding, in his having done what he had to do. She put her hand under his arm and coaxed him to his feet.

"The ponies are getting worried," she said.

He followed her listlessly down the dusty flights; the ponies were stamping fretfully in the shadows, but as much from boredom and strangeness as from fear—or perhaps the stress the children felt was making them kick the cobbles in that fretful way. Jonathan walked up to Caesar and slapped his well-padded shoulder.

"Shut up, you fat idiot," he said. "We could stick it out for months here. Corn for you and pineapples for me and a million rats to talk to."

Caesar enjoyed being spoken to like that. Margaret fondled Scrub's nose and gently teased his ears until he was calm. Then she opened the door. The water was almost still now, though two dogs still paddled feebly at the far edge. A few more shapes floated in the middle of the water—the others must have got out somehow, or sunk when they drowned. As she looked, a hatch on *Heartsease* opened and a cautious head poked out—Lucy's. Margaret stepped into the open and waved; an arm waved back. Jonathan came and stood beside her, with his usual perky, cat-faced look.

"If they used their pole to break the ice around her," he said, "they could cast off the far hawser and we could haul her over."

"Scrub and Caesar could, anyway," said Margaret.

But it took five minutes of signaling and hallooing before Lucy grasped the idea and persuaded Tim to do the work. Meanwhile Margaret devised a makeshift connection between the near hawser and Scrub's horsecollar, and an even more makeshift harness for Caesar to do his share of hauling in. Caesar didn't mind, but the ramshackle and once-only nature of the whole contraption displeased Scrub's conservative soul, and she had to bully him before he suddenly bent to his task like a pit-pony and began to haul the inert but frictionless mass across the dock. Margaret led the ponies back into the warehouse, so that they could pull straight.

"Whoa!" shouted Jonathan from the quayside, and she hauled back on the bridles. The hawser deepened its curve until it lay like a basking snake along the floor, but it was many seconds before she heard the dull boom of the tug nudging up against the stonework. Three minutes later they had shut the ponies back in the warehouse and were standing on the deck, where Tim was cuddling a draggled yellow blob with a snarling black snout.

"What's he got?" said Margaret.

"Puppy," said Lucy. "He fished un off a bit of ice as the boat ran past. Come and see Otto. He's better—in his mind, that is. He can't move his legs still, and his side hurts him, but he's better in his mind."

She led them below.

Chapter 6

WILL SHE GO?

It was glorious to be out of the fingering wind.

The cabin, an odd-shaped chamber with a tilting floor and walls which both curved and sloped, was beautifully warm and stuffy—warm from the round stove which crackled against the inner wall, stuffy from being lived in by three people. The witch lay in a corner, his feet down the slope of the floor, and watched them scramble down the ladder; the reflection of daylight from the open hatch made his eyes gleam bright as a robin's. He looked thin, tired, ill—but not dying, not any longer.

"Welcome to the resistance movement," he said in his strange voice, slow and spoken half through his nose. "What you got there, Tim? Another patient?"

Tim cooed happily and put his bundle on the floor, a wet, yellow, floppy pup, just big enough to have followed its mother with the pack but not big enough to fend for itself, nor to tilt off its patch of ice and drown. It snarled at them all and slashed at Tim's hand; he didn't snatch it away but let the puppy chew at it with sharp little teeth until Lucy handed him a mutton bone. The puppy took it ungraciously into the darkest corner and settled down to a private growling match.

Otto laughed.

"What shall we call him?" he said. "If it is a him."

"Davey," said Margaret without thinking. The other two children looked at her, surprised.

"Means something to you?" said Otto. "Okay, fine. What happened outside? We heard the noises but we couldn't figure them out. At least you won your battle."

Jonathan told him what they had done in dry sentences, as though it had happened to someone else and was not very interesting anyway. Otto listened without a word and then lay silent, twitching his eyes from face to face.

"Yeah," he said at last. "I reckoned I'd just been mighty lucky till now. I didn't know we had a thinker pulling for us."

"We can't do it if we're not lucky," said Jonathan without emphasis.

"Yes," burst in Margaret, "but we couldn't have got anywhere without Jo. He's made all the luck *work.*"

"The question is can we make the engines work," said Jonathan.

"What's she got?" said Otto.

"I think it must be diesel," said Jonathan. "It's very old; there's a brass plate on the engine saying nineteen twenty-eight. I can't see anywhere for a furnace, or for storing coal; and there are feed-pipes which look right for oil and wrong for water, and a big oil tank behind here."

He slapped the partition behind the stove. Otto whistled.

"Nineteen twenty-eight!" he said. "A genuine vintage tub, then. Isn't there anything newer?"

"Yes," said Jonathan, "the other tug, the one that's not sunk I mean, looks much newer and much more complicated. But it's in a mess, as though they were using it all the time just before the Changes came. But this one's very tidy, with everything stowed away and covered up and tied down. I thought perhaps it was so old that they didn't use it at all, but just kept it here, laid up. So they might have left it properly cared for, so that *they'd* be able to start it if they hadn't tried for a long time."

"Yeah," said Otto, "that they might. And another thing—a primitive engine is a simple engine—unsophisticated, not much to go wrong, provided she isn't all seized up. I'll get Tim to lug me along for a look-see as soon as my rib's mended, three more weeks maybe. And where'll you sail us then, captain?"

"We're in Gloucester Docks," said Jonathan. "There's a canal which goes down to the Bristol Channel. Margaret's explored it. It's about fifteen miles long, she thinks, and not many people live near it. The bridges over it open quite easily, though she didn't try them all. There's only one lock, out beyond the other docks at the far end. We thought we'd use the ponies to tow *Heartsease* right down there, and if anyone stopped us we could say it was a wicked machine and we wanted to get it away from our part of the canal—that would be a good argument in England now. And when we got there we could see if we could find enough fuel (or we could look for some here) and see if we can make the lock work. If we can we'll try to start the engines and get out down the Bristol Channel, and if we can't we'll think of something else."

"Sharpness," said Otto. "That's the name of the port at the far end; I remember it from my briefing. And another thing I remember—that the Bristol Channel's just about the trickiest water in Europe. Tide goes belting in and out, six knots each way, and drops thirty foot in two hours; then the river's nothing but mud flats and a bit of stream winding through the middle. We'll need charts."

"I'm hungry," said Margaret.

"Right," said Otto. "Food first, action after. What's on the menu?"

"We've nigh on eaten all you brought last time, Master Jonathan," said Lucy.

"We've brought enough for another three days, I hope," said Margaret.

"Anyway," said Jonathan, "the warehouse is absolutely full of cans."

"Given you can find a can opener," said Otto.

The shape of that forgotten tool was suddenly sharp in Margaret's mind, like an image out of a lost dream.

"I'll look for an ironmonger's," said Jonathan, "after I've burgled the offices for charts."

While they ate the firm cheese and crisp-crusted bread (one thing about Rosie, she baked better than anyone else in the village) they talked a little and thought a lot. Margaret was dismayed to find that they were less than halfway through their job; the most dangerous part was still to come. And she alone knew how huge and immovable-seeming were the steel gates down at Sharpness. She distracted herself from her worries by watching Tim coax the puppy into trusting him, so gentle, so patient that it was difficult to remember that he hadn't all his wits. The puppy was quite wild, but with generations of man-trust bred into it; savagery and hunger and fear fought with these older instincts, sometimes winning, sometimes losing. At last there came a moment when it took a fragment of bacon from Tim's hand without snatching and running away, then stayed where it was to let him rub the back of its skull with his rough, dirty fingers.

She looked around the cabin and saw that the others had been watching just as intently as she had, as though the fall of kingdoms depended on Tim's winning.

"He's not so hungry now," explained Jonathan with his dry laugh.

"Tim, you're marvelous," said Margaret.

"Why do you want to name him after Mr. Gordon,

then, Miss Margaret?" said Lucy, soft and suspicious as
of old.

"I don't know," said Margaret. "Mr. Gordon's a bit
like that, I suppose, savage and doing what he does
because something in him makes him. But I thought it
might be lucky too, I don't know how."

"Who's Mr. Gordon?" said Otto.

It was not comfortable to explain, because if Mr.
Gordon had not lived in the village Otto might never
have been stoned. Even so, they found themselves trying to make as good a case as they could for the terrible
old man, partly for the honor of the village but partly
for reasons they couldn't put a name to.

Otto's good hand kept fingering the puckered tissues
which were left after the healing of his smashed cheek.

"To think of you kids living with all this and staying
like you have," he said when they'd finished.

"It's Aunt Anne, more than anything," explained
Margaret.

"And that's true," whispered Lucy.

Jonathan didn't speak, but got up and climbed the
ladder into the square of daylight. Margaret went with
him and found that the tug had now drifted a few feet
away from the quay. For the first time she really looked
at *Heartsease* by daylight—a dirty old boat, black where it
wasn't rusty, about seventy feet long; the bulwarks
curved out from the uptilted prow about knee-high, and
became shallower as they reached the rounded stern;
the cabin was at the fore end, its roof barely a foot
above deck level; then a narrow strip of deck beneath

which lay the fuel tank; then the wheelhouse, which was really just a windowed shed much too tall and wide for the proportions of the boat. Behind that stood the big funnel, with its silly little hat brim running around it just below the top—she could still see the lines of color which showed which shipping firm the tug had belonged to. The funnel rose from the top of a low, flat roof, along whose side ran tiny rectangular windows, which could only allow the skimpiest ration of light through to whatever was below. The engine room. Under there must lie the iron monster which Jonathan was going to try to wake; it was the monster's weight which set the tug so much down by the stern, making it (even at rest) seem to tilt with an inward energy as though it were crouched to tackle huge seas. And last of all came an open area of deck rounded off by the curve of the bulwarks at the stern. This was what Margaret had been looking for—a place where she could tether Scrub when the time came.

Jonathan had opened the engine room hatch and was kneeling beside it, craning down into the gap, his trousers taut over his rump, his whole body as tense as a terrier at a rat hole. Margaret nudged his ribs with her shoe and he stood up frowning.

"Too difficult for me," he said. "At least, I'm sure I could understand it if Otto would teach me. If you'll show Lucy where the cans are I'll look for charts and a can opener."

"Don't you think Tim had better go with you, just in case?"

Jonathan agreed, and scuttled down into the engine room. He came back with a massive wrench, almost the shape of a caveman's club. Margaret explained to Lucy, who frowned and stood biting her thumb in the cabin. It was difficult for her: danger for Jonathan meant danger for Tim; but they would never get away if Jonathan went into danger alone and was caught by the dogs; and Tim couldn't decide for himself, so . . .

She sighed, shook herself and tried to explain to Tim that he was to go with Jonathan to stop him from being hurt. At last he grasped the idea that something was dangerous, and took the big wrench. Jonathan led him off. Every few yards he brandished the wrench and snarled right and left.

"Do you think he'd actually hit a dog if he had to?" said Margaret.

"I dunno," whispered Lucy, "but he'd surely fright 'em."

She gazed after the hulking back with just the same smile as a mother's who watches her pudgy toddler playing some private game. Margaret had never liked her so much.

The ponies had become fretful in their strange dark stall, all rustling with rats, but it seemed safe enough to lead them out and tether them on the quay. On the first floor of the warehouse Margaret found a sack which seemed not to have gone musty, so she tilted a double helping of corn into the fold of her skirt, carried it down and spread it in two piles on the snow. The ponies sniffed it, then gobbled greedily at it.

By the time the girls had carried their third load of cans aboard, Jonathan and Tim were back, both too laden with looted goods to fight off a single hungry terrier. Luckily they hadn't even met that. They had charts and tide tables, books for Otto, a can opener and knives and forks. Jonathan dumped his load on the deck and opened a blue metal case.

"Look, Marge," he said. "Aren't they *beautiful?*"

There was a wild light in his eyes, as though he had drunk some drug, when all he had found was an expensive tool chest full of shiny wrenches and firm pliers.

When all their treasures were stowed away they said good-bye to Otto, jumped ashore and pushed the tug out along the channel through the ice with a scaffold plank Margaret had found. No dogs barked as they rode away. It was too late to visit Cousin Mary; in fact it was drawing toward dusk when the ponies plodded down the last slope toward the farm, Scrub sulky because he hadn't been far enough and Caesar sulky because he'd been anywhere at all.

That night Margaret had the second of her nightmares about the bull at Splatt Bridge. Two nights later she had the same dream again; again the bull was pelting toward her; again Scrub vanished from beneath her; again she was waist-high in clinging grass, unable to turn or run or cry for help; again she woke with a slamming heart and lay sweating in the dark, telling herself it was only a dream. And the same a few nights later; and twice next week; and so on, for six weeks, while the frost locked hill and vale in its iron grasp.

No more snow fell, but even the sun at noon had no strength to melt what already lay. Where the earth was bare it boomed when you struck it with a stick, as though the whole round world were your drum. Christmas came with carols and trooping into the tomb-cold church to hear a long service in Latin (the parson was sober this year) and cooking big slabs of meat and bread in case the revelers felt hungry while they were shouting in the farmyard (you couldn't call it singing); all the men's faces were cider-purple in the feast-day firelight, but surly and ashamed next morning.

Aunt Anne slowly recovered, and began to eat a little and smile a little, especially when Jonathan was in the room. Mr. Gordon visited them several times, but seemed more like a bent old gossip than a dangerous slayer of witches.

Every third day the children took it in turns to ride down to the docks. They had no need to think of an excuse now, because Cousin Mary's leg was worse and she had taken to her bed. She and Aunt Anne forgave each other the silver teapot, and began to exchange long weepy letters on scraps of hoarded paper, chatting over the adventures of their own girlhood, and the children carried them to and fro. Uncle Peter worked hard and said little. He slept in the kitchen, preferring it to Aunt Anne's sickroom.

Heartsease froze hard into the ice again, twelve feet from the quay. Jonathan found a ladder and raided the ironmonger's for nails, so that when Margaret next rode down she found a bridge between shore and ship which a human could clamber across but a dog couldn't. The pack could have crossed the ice again, of course, but never came—they were scared of the docks now, and no wonder.

But Jonathan had hit trouble in the business of clearing the towpath down to Hempsted Bridge. Not one gate, but several, blocked it, where different industrial estates had sealed off their own territories. He toiled away steadily with looted crowbars and hacksaws and blot-cutters. He also found two or three inlets of water on that side: they would have to get enough way on *Heartsease* to let her drift past while they led Scrub around the edge.

In the middle of January, Margaret found that Otto had been moved into the engine room. Reluctantly she climbed down iron rungs into a chilly chamber whose whole center was occupied by a great gray mass of iron, bulging into ponderous cylinders, flowering with taps and dials. Otto's bed was in the narrow gangway which ran all around it. There was a much smaller engine outside the gangway on either side.

"Did you ever see anything like it?" he said. "It's so primitive it ought to be made of flint. A Dutch diesel, my pop would have called it—they used to have tractors like it when he was a kid. See those things on top of the cylinders that look like blowlamps? You light 'em up and let 'em blow onto the cylinder heads; then you get the auxiliary going—that's this motor here; we won't need the other one, it's only electric—and pump up the air bottles, over yonder. Then, when the cylinder heads are good and hot, you turn on the fuel, give her a blast of compressed air from the bottles and she's going. Got it?"

"No," said Margaret. "It's not the sort of thing I understand. But *will* it go?"

"Tim's turned her over for me, and the parts all move. So far so good, that's the best you can say. But I can't see why she shouldn't."

"Have you told Jo?"

"Uh-huh," said Otto. "He's fallen in love with her, I reckon."

"You won't let him touch it, will you?" said Margaret urgently. "Not until we're ready to go?"

"Why so?"

"Otherwise he'll get himself all covered with rust and oil and begin to smell of machines. And even if he doesn't actually *smell,* Mr. Gordon will nose him out."

"This Mr. Gordon," said Otto, "I'm beginning to think he's a bit of a baddie. If he was a cowboy he'd wear a black hat."

"It isn't like that," said Margaret. "Nobody's like that. It's all caused by things which happened long ago, long ago, and probably no one noticed when they happened. I don't even know if he was always a cripple—I must ask Uncle Peter."

Otto stared at her for a long time. Then he said, "Forget it—I was only joking."

"I'm sorry," said Margaret. "I didn't understand. We aren't used to jokes in our world."

"Okay," said Otto, "I'll keep your Jonathan away, best I can, but his fingers are itching."

"I'll talk to him. Is there a lot to do to the engine?"

"Injectors to be cleaned is the main thing," said Otto. "That's them on top. Lucy can do it, if she can show Tim how to loosen 'em off."

Lucy gave a funny little bubble of laughter over in her corner.

"When I go to heaven," she said, "there won't be no cleaning. I spent four years cleaning the farmhouse, and then I'm cleaning Otto, and now I'm going to clean a hulking great lump of iron."

"Sweetie," said Otto, "if we get home I'll see to it that the United States government buys you a dishwasher, three clothes washers and eighteen floor polishers."

"I should like that," said Lucy.

That night Margaret gave Jonathan a long, whispered sermon about staying away from machines. He made a comic disappointed face, but nodded. Then, after his next visit, he crept into the kitchen reeking of a heady, oily smell. Luckily Uncle Peter was out, tending a sick heifer. Margaret took Jonathan's clothes and poked them one by one into the back of the fire, which roared strangely as it bit into them; and she made Jonathan take a proper, all-over bath in front of the hearth. They had just tilted the water out down the pantry drain when there was a rattle at the bolted door—Rosie, back from calling on her cousin. She sniffed sharply around the kitchen the moment she was in.

"Funny kind of whiff in here," she said.

"I fell in a bog," said Jonathan.

"Fool of a boy," said Rosie. "Give me your clothes and I'll put 'em to soak."

"I've burned them," said Margaret. "They smelled awful—I think there must have been something wicked in the bog."

"Nice to be rich folk," said Rosie sharply. "Some might say wasteful."

"I'll ask Mr. Gordon, shall I?" said Margaret. "He'd know if I was right."

"Maybe," said Rosie, and went sniffing upstairs.

Jonathan winked at Margaret from his swathing towels, but she was shivering with the nearness of the escape. Later, when they went out to water the ponies, he explained that he had checked the fuel on *Heartsease* and there was plenty of diesel oil but not enough kerosene for the blowlamps on top of the cylinders; he'd found some drums of the stuff in a shed, but the one he tried to roll outside had been so rusted through that it split and spilled all over him. Margaret tried to scold him, but already he was talking excitedly about something called the bilge, which he'd shown Tim how to empty; the point was that the tug had hardly leaked at all.

Next time Margaret visited the docks Lucy was sitting with a piece of dirty machinery in her lap, swabbing at it with a clear, smelly liquid, the same that Jonathan had reeked of—kerosene. Margaret ran up the ladder again, fearful that the stink of the stuff would get into her hair. Tim was on deck, carefully cleaning his way around with a brush; the puppy, Davey, crouched watchfully beside

him and as soon as he had gathered a little mound of
rustflakes and dirt would leap on it with a happy wuff
and scatter it around the deck. Luckily Tim enjoyed the
game too, and seemed prepared to go on all day,
sweeping and then seeing his work undone. But between games (perhaps while Davey was snoozing) the
tug had become cleaner; the windows of the wheelhouse had been wiped, too, and the bigger flakes of
peeling paint removed. But to set against this tidiness
there was a nasty little pyramid of used cans on the ice
under the bows—Lucy's style.

Margaret knew that she herself would have carried
them out of sight, but she couldn't any longer despise
Lucy for not doing things her way. And if she wasn't
going to nag there was nothing for her to do, so she
called her good-byes down the hatch and was answered
by two preoccupied mumbles, Lucy busy with her cleaning and Otto with his charts and tide tables. Scrub had
never learned to approve of the docks and walked off
briskly the moment she was mounted.

Cousin Mary was much worse, too poorly even to
write; she raised her fat hulk onto an elbow to give
Margaret a few word-of-mouth messages to Aunt Anne,
but almost at once sank back sweating with pain. Even
having someone in the room obviously tired her. Margaret left quickly.

They were trotting up the lane toward the main road
when Scrub suddenly faltered into a limping walk. Margaret jumped down and saw that he was shifting his off
foreleg in obvious distress; when she lifted the hoof she

found a ball of snow packed like iron inside it, which it took her several minutes to pry out. The other three hooves were nearly as bad. She straightened when she had cleared them and looked at the landscape with new eyes: the ash by the lane was dripping its own private rainfall onto the pocked snow beneath; the wind smelled of the warm sea and not of the icy hills; there was a tinkling in the ditch beneath the crust of snow. The whole Vale was thawing, thawing fast.

She had to clear Scrub's hooves twice more before they reached the first house in Edge, where a tiny woman lent her enough lard to smear into them to stop the gluey snow from sticking.

Jonathan was so fidgety with excitement that evening that Rosie kept looking at him with the sour glance of someone who is being kept out of a secret. Margaret knew what he was thinking: He had only two more gates across the towpath to demolish. In a few days the canal, too, would be clear, and they could tow the tug down, by stages, to Sharpness and work out how the lock gates functioned and watch the pattern of the tides. He chattered about it next morning when they were picking up the eggs, their whispers safe from inquisitive ears amid the scuttling and clucking of disturbed hens.

"Jo," she said in a pause, "I don't want to come with you."

He looked up with a puckered stare from groping under the nesting box where Millicent always hid her egg.

"Why not?"

"I'm frightened. Not of the journey, or what people will do if they catch us. I'm frightened of that too, of course, but it's different. I'll help you get away, but then I want to come back here."

He stood up and sighed.

"You can't," he said. "Mr. Gordon—all of them—will know you were in it. Think what they'll do then. You'll have made fools of them."

She stared at the straw until it grew misty; then she shook her head to clear the half-started tears. Jonathan bent to search for Millicent's hidden treasure again.

"We'll find room for Scrub," he said without looking at her.

It seemed a long week before it was her turn to ride down again. The farmyard became mushy, the fields squelched, the ditches gushed and the millstream at the bottom roared with melting snow. A slight frost most nights slowed the thaw up, but when at last she headed Scrub down into the Vale the only snow lay in wavering strips along the northern side of walls and hedges. She dismounted at the bridge and prodded the ice with a stick; there was an inch of water above it, and it gave way when she pushed—it would be gone next day. On *Heartsease* the engine was fitted together again and Otto was reading *Oliver Twist*. Lucy was cooking on the cabin stove, hemmed in by the piles of tools and rope and tackle and oddments which Jonathan had been looting from deserted ironmongers' and ships' chandlers. Tim was exercising Davey on the quayside. There was nothing for her to do again, except to warn them to be ready for the slow, three-day tow to Sharpness. Already they all seemed to have settled into such a routine of danger that she was hardly worried by the thought of that stretch of the adventure: it all ought to be quite straightforward, she thought. They could simply pick their time.

But when she rode into Hempsted there was a funeral cart at Cousin Mary's door. Their excuse for visiting the Vale was gone.

Chapter 7

ENGINES

Jonathan thought for almost a minute, biting the back of his knuckle while his breath steamed in the early moonlight. Then he picked up his side of the big bucket and helped her edge it through the paddock gate and tilt the water into the trough.

"I'll ride down tomorrow night," he said, "and warn them to get ready. Then we can both go down two nights after that and start the towing in the dark. We'll be halfway to Sharpness before they even miss us, and they'll never guess which way we've gone."

"We must say good-bye to Aunt Anne somehow," said Margaret.

"I'll write her a letter. I'll do it tomorrow so that I don't have to do it at the last minute, and I'll hide it in

my room. Cheer up, Marge, she'll feel better when
we've gone because she'll stop worrying about us.
That's why she's been so ill, knowing what'd happen to
us if we're found."

"But she doesn't know what we're doing," said Margaret.

"She knows we're doing something, though."

Margaret remembered the haggard face, and the
bony hands that had banged her to and fro in bed.

"Yes," she said.

He was in his room all next afternoon, toiling away
(Margaret knew) at his half-taught, baby-big handwrit-
ing. He would tell Aunt Anne everything, too, because
she had a right to know the truth, a right to know the
real reasons why he had to go. Margaret went to bed
feeling guilty in the awareness that he was keeping himself awake so that when the house was still he could
climb out and ride the tiring journey down to their
companions; but she was quickly asleep. Perhaps she
stirred and frowned when the board outside on the
landing creaked as someone trod on it in the darkness,
or perhaps the stirring and frowning were caused by the
first waves of terror as she began on the old, horrible
dream about the bull.

But this time the dream never finished. Instead she
was wide awake, staring at darkness, heart slamming,
because something out of the real world had woken her
—a shouting and stamping on the stairs, three hammer-
ing paces on the landing, and the door of her room
opening like a thunderclap. Uncle Peter towered there,

a lantern in one hand and in the other several sheets of paper, all different sizes.

"What's this? What's this?" he bellowed, and shoved the papers under her nose. She put out a hand to take them, though she knew quite well what they were, but he snatched them away. His face was so tense with rage that she could have counted the different muscles of his cheeks. Rosie hovered in the doorway behind him.

"What's what?" quavered Margaret—no matter how scared she sounded, because she would have been scared even if she'd known nothing.

"A letter!" he shouted. "A letter to your aunt! Jo wrote it. Says he rescued that witch and he's going to get him away from Gloucester Docks in a filthy wicked boat! What *d'you* know about it, my girl?"

"Where did you find it?" asked Margaret in a wobbly voice.

"Rosie brought it to me," he growled. Rosie's acid tones took over.

"I was leaning on my sill," she said, "looking out at the night, when I saw Master Jonathan ride away into the dark of the lane. So I puzzled what he might be about, and went along to his room to see if there was nothing there to tell, and sure enough I found this letter, so I took it to the master. No more than my duty, was it?"

"No," said Margaret. "I'm sure you did right. Have you told Aunt Anne, Uncle Peter?"

"None of your business!" he shouted, so she knew he

hadn't. "He talks about *we*—we did this, we're planning that. *You're* in it!"

"Oh, no, Uncle Peter! You can't think that. I don't know anything about machines—I hate them and I wouldn't understand them anyway. Don't you think he might mean Lucy and Tim?"

Uncle Peter peered for a moment at the paper, too dazed with anger to read or think. Then he shoved his face close against Margaret's, so that she could smell his cabbagy breath, and stared into her eyes.

"Maybe," he growled deep in his throat, "maybe not —we'll know the morning. He says he's not planning to be off these two days, so likely he'll be back by dawn. Till then I'll just lock you in while I go and rout Davey Gordon out. Rosie can watch out of the parlor window, so there'll be no nonsense like you tying your sheets together and climbing down, see!"

"Of course not!" said Margaret.

He took his face away and stood brooding for a moment at the lantern.

"Dear Lord in Heaven," he said softly, "have I not been tried enough?"

When he'd gone, followed by Rosie, she sat in the dark pierced through and through with pure despair. First she thought, if I stay where I am it'll look as though I had nothing to do with it. Second, and much stronger, came the thought, I must warn them—if I dress I might just be able to get down from the window and run to Scrub before Rosie catches me. I'll have to ride him bareback, because there'll be no time to harness him, and I doubt if he'll like that, but it's the only chance.

She was putting a big jersey on and still trying to think of a way to distract Rosie from the parlor window when the door scraped faintly—the bolt was being drawn back. Margaret stiffened at the creak of the hinges; now she was going to be caught fully dressed, with no possible lie to account for it.

"Marge, Marge," whispered Aunt Anne's voice, "get dressed as quick as you can."

"I am dressed."

"Oh, thank heavens. He was too angry to think of locking your pony up. You've just time to saddle up and ride to warn Jo. I'll keep Rosie busy while you get through the kitchen."

"No," said Margaret, "I'll climb down from Jo's window—she can't see that side of the house. Then you can bolt the door after me and go back to bed and seem too sick to move, and they won't know what's happened."

"Marge, please, Marge," said Aunt Anne, "if the Changes ever end, bring him home."

"He'll come anyway," said Margaret. "I'm sure."

"And Marge, remember Pete's a *good* man, really. A very good man."

"I know. I like him too."

As she tiptoed down the passage she heard a noise like sobbing, but so faint that the grate of the closing bolt drowned it.

Scrub was waiting for her at the paddock gate, as if there was nothing he wanted more than a midnight gallop. As she tightened the girth of the heavy sidesaddle she heard a new noise in the night—men's excited voices. That meant the lane was blocked, so she swung herself into the saddle and set Scrub's head to the low place in the far wall, which she'd often eyed as a possible jump if it hadn't meant going over into Farmer Boothroyd's land. But tonight she didn't care a straw for old and foolish feuds.

Scrub must have thought about the jump too, for he took it with a clean swoop, like a rook in the wind. Then came a good furlong down across soft and silent turf to the far gate; then the muddy footpath along the bottom of Squire's Park; a steep track up, and they were out in Edge Lane.

Potholed tarmac, unmended through five destroying winters, is a poor surface for a horse to hurry over in the dark, especially when it tilts down like a slate roof between tall hedges. In places Margaret could risk a trot, for they both knew the road well by now, but mostly there was nothing for it but a walk. Luckily Scrub had sensed the excitement and urgency of the journey, so he didn't loiter; but the dip to the stream was agonizingly slow and the climb beyond slower still. Then they could canter along the old main road—though they nearly fell from overconfidence in the pitchy blackness beneath the trees; the descent to the Vale was slow again, before they could hit a really fast clip along the bottom.

Margaret did sums. Caesar was a slower pony, and Jonathan wouldn't be hurrying as much as she was. But he'd left at least an hour before she had—probably two hours. Suppose he spent half an hour at the docks, making arrangements (he'd have thought it all out in his head on the way down, and would know exactly what he wanted)—she'd gain at least half an hour on him on the journey, almost a whole hour; so they'd meet on the big road at the bottom, or the bridge, or the towpath if he'd dallied. She began to strain her ears for distant hooves. The far cry of a dog made her shiver with sudden terror, but it might have been miles away.

The iron bridge rang beneath Scrub's shoes, but that was the only sound in the wide night. She must have missed him; he'd found some clever way home, across fields. Desperately she hurried Scrub along the matted grass of the towpath, leaning low over his neck and peering forward for the place where they turned up past the deserted house into the road.

"Marge!" called a voice out of the shadows behind her. She reined back; hooves scuffled, and a small shape led a larger shape out into the unshadowed path behind her.

"I thought it must be you," said Jonathan. "What's happened?"

"Rosie found your letter and took it to Uncle Peter."

"But I hid . . . Oh, never mind. It all depends what they do. We'd best go back to the tug and talk to the others."

They led the ponies through the ruined garden.

"If they come down here and find us," mused Jonathan, "we'll be done. We could run away, but we'd have to leave Otto, and Tim will be hard to hide. We could turn the horses loose and all hide in the city, but then we'd be worse off than before. But if we can start the engine, and if the canal is deep all the way down, we can get clear away, provided they don't try to cut us off. In a chase we'll go faster than they do, and keep going, and that should give us about two hours at Sharpness. That would be enough if the tide's right, and Otto's worked a tide table out. We'll have to see."

"Couldn't we start to tow her down while you're working on the engines?" said Margaret. "That would save time."

"Not worth it. We've got to run the auxiliary for at least an hour before we can start the main engine, and if we try to do that while we're towing through the countryside people will come swarming out and catch us helpless. Once we go, we must go fast, because of the noise. But you'll still be useful, you two."

She could hear from his voice that he was grinning in the dark.

"You'll have to ride ahead and open the bridges," he said.

"Yes, I think I can do that; nobody lives near them, except for the two at that village down at the far end."

"It's called Purton on the map. We might be able to stop and tow her past there. You're going to have to ride fast, Marge—she does nearly ten miles an hour, flat out, Otto thinks."

"That's too fast. We could do it for a bit, but we'd never keep it up."

"I'll talk to Otto," said Jonathan.

The tug lay still and lightless, a dull black blob on the shiny black water, but Davey yapped once, sharply, as they came along the quay. They heard a quick scuffle as Jonathan crossed the ladder—Tim, presumably holding the muzzle of a struggling pup.

"It's all right," said Jonathan's cheerful voice, pitched just right for everyone to hear, "it's me again."

The scuffling started again, then stopped with the ludicrous gargle of a dog who has been all set to bark and finds there is no need. The hatch from the cabin, where Lucy slept amid Jonathan's loot, rose.

"Forgotten summat, Master Jonathan?" said her soft purr. "Why, you've a body with you, Miss Margaret is it? There's trouble, then?"

"I think it'll be all right, Lucy, provided we start tonight. Father found the letter I wrote to Mother."

Lucy came swiftly out of the hatch and looked into his face.

"And I'll lay he took it straight up to Mus' Gordon," she said.

"Yes, he did," said Margaret.

"I must take Tim away, then," said Lucy.

"You can if you want to," said Jonathan, "but I'm going to try and start the engines and run down to Sharpness. It's sixteen miles, so we should do it in three hours. If we get the engines going just before dawn I'll be able to see to steer, and Marge can ride ahead and scout and open the bridges. You'll be no worse off if you have to run from Sharpness than from Gloucester."

"I've been looking at them maps," said Lucy. "If they've a morsel of sense they'll head to one of the bridges halfway down and catch us there."

"Yes, I've thought of that," said Jonathan, "but it's not their style. I said in my letter we weren't going for two days, so they'll wait for us to come home tonight, and when we don't they'll come blinding down here in the morning. If we get a start we'll be far away by the time they reach here. You think it out while I talk to Otto; if you still want to leave us, you should go at once, but we won't need to start the auxiliary for another two hours."

"I don't like it, neither way," whispered Lucy, and settled chin in hand on the bulwarks.

"You go and lie in her bed, Marge," said Jonathan. "I shan't need you until dawn."

"What about the ponies?"

"Tie them up on the quay. I'll keep an eye on them."

"Scrub's all taut inside—he knows something's up. He needs a roll."

"Oh, goodness!" said Jonathan angrily. "He'll have to roll on cobbles, then."

Margaret scrambled across the bridge, thinking so that's why Caesar is such a broody and difficult character—Jo's never understood him. All horses get tense, after any sort of expedition, and need to work it off, to unwind. She tethered them side by side to a rusty ring set in the quay, fetched Tim's bailing pan and a bucket, and dredged up nasty oily water from the dock for them to drink. She fondled Scrub's neck for a while to calm him, tried to be nice to Caesar (who sneered sulkily back) and crossed the ladder again. The blankets were warm and Lucy-smelling, but the boards beneath them were so hard that they seemed to gnaw at her hip— small chance of going to sleep; but in a minute she was in the middle of a busy dream, senseless with shifting scenes and people who changed into other people, all hurrying for an urgent reason which was never explained to her.

She was woken by clamor for the second time that night. But now it was not Uncle Peter roaring up the stairs, but a noise which England hadn't heard for five years, fuel exploding inside cylinders to bang the pistons up and send the crankshaft whanging around—the auxiliary engine pumping air into the big storage bottles, to provide the pressure which would start the main diesel.

On deck, light glimmered through the glass roof over the engine, a new light whose nature she didn't remember. She knelt at the hatch and peered in: on top of each of the tall cylinders a roaring flame spread across the metal; the auxiliary clattered away; Jonathan was walking down the narrow gangway by the engine peering at the blowlamps—in their light she could see a smear of oil down both his cheeks, like war paint. He must have felt the cold air when she raised the hatch, for he glanced up and gestured to show that he was coming out in a moment. She still felt the repugnance against engines which had been half her thinking life, so she moved away and sat on the bulwarks, looking at the

clifflike warehouses which at this chill hour loomed so
black that even the night sky seemed pale. It was pale,
too. The stars were fewer and smaller. Soon they would
fade, and the tug would rumble out through that
strange interworld between dark and day.

Jonathan, reeking of engines, came and plumped
himself down beside her. She could feel his nerves
humming with the happiness of action.

"All set," he said. "Tim and Lucy are staying.
They've brought a load of cans out of the warehouse,
and a couple of sacks of corn for the ponies. Scrub
won't mind canal water, will he? It's less oily outside the
docks. And I've found four drums which we can fill for
the sea journey—it oughtn't to be more than a day to
Ireland."

"What do you want me to do?" said Margaret.

"Two things, one easy and one difficult. The easy one
is help start the engines. The difficult one is scout ahead
and get the bridges open. That *could* be tricky. You
see—"

"*Must* I help with the engines?" said Margaret.

There was just enough light flickering through the
engine room roof to show how he looked at her, sideways and amused, but kind.

"Not if you don't want to," he said. "But we won't be
able to manage if you don't do the bridges. I've just
done the first one—it was different from the others—
hydraulic—but I managed."

"I'll do the bridges."

"I've got two good maps of the whole canal—they

were pinned up in offices—so we can each have one. Otto and I are going to aim for about six knots—nearly seven miles an hour—because you won't be able to keep ahead if we try to do more. That means we'll have something to spare if we're chased, provided we don't pile up a wave in front of us down the canal. You'll have to average a fast trot."

"The towpath's quite flat, except for one bit," said Margaret. "We should be able to do that."

"It's not as easy as it sounds, because you'll be stopping at the bridges. And you'll have to go carefully around the bends, especially the ones just before the bridges, in case you gallop into trouble. I found a bolt of red flannel which I've cut some squares off for you to take. If there's something wrong you can go back a bit and tie a square to a bush by the bank, so that we've time to stop. If it's something serious, Caesar will have to tow us through."

"He'll get terribly sore. He hasn't worn a collar for years."

"Poor old Caesar," said Jonathan, as though it didn't matter. "He'll have to put up with it. I think that story will work, provided they haven't spotted the smoke."

"Smoke?"

"You'll see. I want to start in quarter of an hour. You could go on now and get well ahead, if you like."

"I'd better wait and help you get Caesar aboard. He won't fancy it."

"How do you know?"

"Like you know about engines."

"Well, let's try now."

Margaret was right. They climbed ashore, took the ladder away and slowly pulled *Heartsease* toward the quay until she lay flush against the stonework, her deck about two feet below the level where they were standing. Jonathan untied Caesar's reins and led him toward the boat, but one pace from the edge of the quay the pony jibbed and hoicked backward, so that Jonathan almost fell over. Then Margaret tried, more gently, with much coaxing and many words; she got him right to the brim before he shied away.

"I hate horses," said Jonathan.

"Let's see if Scrub will do it," said Margaret. She crossed to her own pony, untied him, pulled his ears, slapped his shoulders and led him toward the boat. He, too, stopped at the very verge. Then, with a resigned waggle of his head and a you-know-best snort, he stepped down onto the ironwork deck. Caesar lumbered down at once, determined not to be left alone in this stone desert. Margaret tied his reins to an iron ring in the deck, poured out a generous feed of corn for him and led Scrub ashore. Before she could mount there came a thin cry from the engine room.

"They're ready!" cried Jonathan. "Come and see!"

He scuttled down the ladder. Margaret knelt by the hatch and peered down to where the weird lamps flared with a steady roaring, while the auxiliary battered away at the night. Lucy was standing down at the far end, by the two further cylinders, her hands on a pair of cast-iron turncocks just above shoulder level. Margaret could see two nearer ones—*she* ought to have been standing there. Otto lay in the corner directly below her, and Jonathan made signs to him through the racket, meaning that he would do Margaret's job as well as his own. He pulled briefly at a lever beside the nearest cylinder, and a spout of oily black smoke issued from the four cylinders, just below the turncocks. He glanced around at Otto, who raised the thumb of his left hand. Jonathan pulled hard down on the lever and left it down. There was a deep, groaning thud, followed at once by another, and another, and the whole tug began to vibrate as though two giants were stumping up and down on its deck. Lucy was already twisting her turncocks when Jonathan pranced around beside her and started twisting his. The beat of the heavy pistons steadied; the roaring flames at their heads died away. Margaret straightened up from the clamorous pit and saw a slow cloud of greasy blackness boiling up from the funnel. When she looked back, Jonathan was already halfway up the iron ladder; she made way for him.

"Like a dream!" he shouted.

"What now?" said Margaret. She wanted to get off the boat as soon as she could.

"Lucy will stay down there, to set the engine to the speed I signal for. I'll steer from the wheelhouse. You move off and open the first bridge. We'll follow in five minutes, and you ought to be nearly at the second one by then."

Margaret stood quite still. She knew there was some-

thing in the plan that didn't fit. She was just turning
away when it came to her.

"Some of the bridges open from the wrong side!" she
said urgently. "I'll have to wait till you're through and
shut them before I can ride on."

Jonathan shut his eyes, as though he was trying to
draw the mechanism on the back of his eyelids.

"I'm a fool," he said at last. "They seemed so simple
that I didn't really think about them. We'll have to go
slower and let you catch up."

"Let's see how we get on," said Margaret, and swung
herself up into the saddle. She was cold, and there was a
scouring northwest wind beginning to slide across the
Vale, the sort of wind that clears the sky to an icy paleness, and keeps you glancing into the eye of the wind
for the first signs of the storm that is sure to follow. But
in the shelter of the docks the water was still the color of
darkest laurel leaves, and smooth as a jewel.

Behind her the beat of the engines deepened. It was
surprising how quiet they were, she thought, once you
were a few yards away. But when she looked around she
saw, black against the paling sky, the wicked stain of the
diesel smoke. If it's going to be like that all the way, she
thought, we'll rouse the whole Vale. But even as she
watched in the bitter breeze the smoke signal changed;
the black plume thinned and drifted away, and in its
place the funnel began to emit tidy black puffs, like the
smoke over a railway engine in a child's drawing; the
wind caught the puffs and rubbed them out before they
had risen ten feet—not so bad, after all.

This last time she decided to risk going right through Hempsted village, instead of dismounting and leading Scrub down through the difficult track to the canal. They'd always gone by the towpath and the empty house before, in case any of the Hempsted villagers should become inquisitive about their comings and goings. But now it wouldn't matter anymore. Hempsted slept as she cantered through. This was one of the bridges that opened from the easy side; she lifted the two pieces of iron that locked the bridge shut and cranked the whole structure open; it moved like magic, with neither grate nor clank.

If she had been good at obeying orders she would have mounted and ridden on, but she felt she owed something to the villagers of Hempsted, though she couldn't say what. At least they had left the children to work out their plot in peace—and that man *had* tried to warn her about the dogs. So she couldn't leave them cut off, bridgeless (no one would care to shut a wicked bridge like this, even if they could remember how). Besides, she wanted to watch *Heartsease* come through.

Jonathan slowed down the engines and shouted something from the wheelhouse as the tug surged past, but she waved to show she knew what she was doing, and swung the bridge slowly (how slowly!) back to its proper place. She heard the beat of the engines quickening and saw the black cloud boil up again. Just as she was bending to put the first locking-bar back she heard a shout. Without looking to see who it was, she slung herself into the saddle, shook the reins, and let Scrub whisk her onto the towpath. Now, over her shoulder, she saw a little old man in a nightshirt standing at the other end of the bridge shaking a cudgel. She waved cheerfully back.

Heartsease was already around the next bend when Margaret caught up, the funnel still puffing its ridiculous smoke rings against the pearly light of dawn, the throaty boom coming steadily from the huge cylinders. She was surprised to find, as she cantered level with the boat, that even she felt an odd pride and thrill at the sense of total strength which the shape of the boat gave because of the way it sat in the water. She slowed to a trot to watch it.

At once Jonathan moved his hand on the brass lever that jutted up beside the wheel; the boom of the engines altered; *Heartsease,* no longer shoved by the propellers, began to lose speed as Jonathan edged her in toward the bank. He opened the door of the wheelhouse.

"It'll be all right," he called, "provided you can keep that sort of speed up. You must think of a story, just in case you're caught on the wrong side with a bridge open. What about . . ."

"They wouldn't believe it," Margaret interrupted. "We'll just have to swim. That old stableboy who came when the earl came told me horses can swim with a grown man on them. But Jo, try to keep your engine going the same speed all the time. It makes a horrid black cloud when you speed up. People could see it for miles, but you can't in there."

"Thanks!" said Jonathan. He shut his door, signaled down to Lucy in the engine room, and, as the water churned behind the tug's stern and the black smoke rose again, steered out for the center of the canal. Scrub was happy to go. The wind was even colder now, out from the sheltering buildings.

Scrub was in good form, happy with the tingling early morning air and the excitement of having something to do. Margaret was sure he knew how much it mattered, that he sensed her own thrill and urgency. The towpath was a good surface, hard and flat underneath but overlaid with rank fallen grasses which softened the fall of his feet. She had to rein him in firmly as they took the bend at the end of the long straight, and he was fidgeting with the bit all the three hundred yards down to the next bend. Just around it was another bridge. This one opened from the wrong side.

Already it was almost a routine, she thought as she hitched the reins to the rail, hoicked up the locking-piece and began to crank. But as the bridge swung over the water there was a shrill burst of barking in the lane behind her.

Margaret panicked. In a flash she had untied the reins, flung herself up to the saddle and hauled Scrub around to set him up at the awkward jump from the end of the bridge to the bank. It wasn't impossibly far, but it was all angles. He took it as though he'd been practicing for weeks, and climbed up to the towpath. From there Margaret looked back.

The smallest dog she had ever seen, very scrawny and
dirty, was yelping in the entrance to the far lane.

Jonathan had slowed *Heartsease* down, but even so the
tug was almost at the bridge, and there was no way for
Margaret to cross and finish her job. She was turning
Scrub toward the bitter water, nerving herself for the
shock of cold, when she looked up the canal and saw her
cousin gesticulating in the wheelhouse—he had another plan, and he didn't want them to swim.

His hand moved to the big brass signal lever and
pulled it right over. The tug surged on for a second,
and then there was a boiling of yellow water beneath
the stern as the propeller went into reverse. *Heartsease*
suddenly sat differently, slowed, wavered and was
barely moving, drifting through the water, nudging
with a mild thud against the concrete pier on Margaret's
side of the gap. The bridges were still high at this end of
the canal, because the surrounding land was high: it was
only the mast and the funnel which wouldn't slide under. Delicately, with short bursts of power from the
propeller, Jonathan sidled round the projecting arm,
just scraping the corner of the wheelhouse as they went
past. Once through, he opened the wheelhouse door to
lean back and watch the oily smoke fade as *Heartsease*
settled down to her six-knot puff-puff-puff.

"Sorry!" shouted Margaret. "I was too frightened to
think."

"Not surprised," he shouted back. "But it looked
funny from here—you two great animals routed by that

little rat of a dog. Couldn't you lean down and turn the handles from the saddle?"

"No. They're too low. How far is it to the next bridge? Scrub doesn't understand about maps—the flapping makes him nervous."

"Half a mile. Then a mile and a half to the one after. Get ahead and come up to that one carefully, just trotting along. There used to be an inn there, and more folk'll be about by now."

The next bridge opened from the right side and no one barked or shouted at her. Then came the stretch of bad towpath, all muddy hummocks, so she took to the fields and cantered along on the wrong side of the hedge, wondering why the canal wasn't all in that kind of condition. The answer came to her at once, as she pictured the boiling khaki wake behind *Heartsease*. No ships had been using the canal for five years, so the water had barely moved; it had been when large engines had churned the surface about that the banks had needed constant looking after.

As she came up toward Sellers Bridge and the inn beside it, she settled Scrub to his easiest trot, and made sure that there was a square of red cloth loose at the top of her saddlebag.

She remembered the pub from her first exploration —a large white square building with broken windows. It hadn't looked as if anyone lived there, but she slowed to a casual trot as a gentle curve brought the bridge into view. The whole narrow world—the world between the enclosing banks of the canal—seemed empty of people, but who could say what enemies mightn't be about beyond them? As she wound at the handle she felt the blank windows of the ruined inn watching her, she felt the vast silence of the Vale listening like a spy to the slow clack of the cogs beneath her. This bridge was slightly different from the others: even though it opened from the "good" end, it turned on a pivot so that when it was open she was left with an awkward leap down to the bank. She decided it was safer to close it, but by the time she had watched *Heartsease* pass and had cranked the bridge shut she was shivery and sweating.

The next bridge was already open, and now the land fell away on either side of her so that she could feel the teeth of the wind out of Wales—and the banks would no longer hide the tug. Now they would be parading their wicked engine before all the watching Vale, twenty miles wide. At the bridge after that all went well, though it opened from the wrong side, but as Margaret was cantering on she heard a shrill cry and looked back to see a woman brandishing a saucepan while an arthritic old man hobbled away down the lane—for help, probably, for somebody young and strong to pursue them. Margaret bent over Scrub's neck and let him stretch to a full gallop; she was sure they could outrun any pursuit, provided they weren't halted in their flight. Hungry, she felt into her saddlebag as soon as they were past the tug, and found a hunk of Rosie's bread to gnaw.

It was two miles to the next bridge, a flimsy affair for foot traffic, where the canal crossed the narrow little barge canal from Stroud, all reeded and silted. Then a

short stretch to Sandfield Bridge, which opened from
the "good" side; then nearly a mile more to the bridge
between Frampton and Saul. That one lay amid brooding woods which screened the next expanse of country,
and it was already open. Frampton, she remembered,
lay only a furlong from the canal, and beyond the
woods was a long straightaway through windswept and
shelterless country; so, as she was now well ahead of the
tug, she took Scrub down the embankment, dismounted and led him along by the overgrown gardens
of Saul Lodge. The canal here ran ten feet higher than
the land. She was completely under cover as she walked
below the stretching arms of the pine trees to a point,
thirty yards on, where the curve was finished and she
could climb up again until only her head showed as she
spied out the long straightaway.

For five endless seconds she peered around a clump
of withered nettle stems.

Then she had wrenched the startled pony around and
was running back along the awkward slope. Up onto the
path the moment it might be safe; into the saddle; galloping back and reaching at the same moment for the
square of red cloth. *Heartsease* was only fifty yards the
other side of the open bridge; desperately she waved
her danger signal.

The water creamed under the stern as the propeller
clawed at it to slow the tug down, but already they were
through the bridge and Margaret could see that the
momentum would take the tug around the curve before
she could be stopped. Jo twirled the wheel and the bow

swung toward the towpath; two seconds later it slid into the bank with a horrid thud. She jumped from her pony and ran along the path, but before she came to the place the still-churning engine had lugged the boat out into midstream again. Jonathan moved the lever to the stop position and opened the wheelhouse door.

"I hope that was worth it," he called.

"Oh, Jo, we're done for! Come and see! Can you turn the engine off without making smoke?"

He fiddled with the lever and the wheel, so that a quick spasm of power sucked *Heartsease* backward to lie against the bank. Margaret caught the rope he threw and tied it to a thornbush; he scuttled down the engine room hatch, and almost at once the puff-puff-puff from the funnel died away. Lucy came up behind him, her face all mottled with oil and dirt, but stayed on the deck while he leaped ashore. Caesar fidgeted with his tether in the stern.

Margaret led Jonathan along under the embankment. The children peered again around the hissing nettle stems, down the mile-long line of water which rippled grayly in the sharp wind, to where Splatt Bridge sat across the dismal surface like a black barricade.

There were people on the bridge, about a dozen of them, tiny with distance but clearly visible in the wide light of the estuary. Above them rose a spindly framework with a hunched blob in the middle.

"What on earth have they got there?" said Jonathan.

"Mr. Gordon's litter."

Chapter 8

KNIFE AND ROPE

There was no mistaking it. The freshening northwester had cleared every trace of haze from the fawn-and-silver landscape.

"Bother," said Jonathan. "It's strange how you never expect other people to be as clever as you are yourself."

He spoke in an ordinary voice, but looking at him Margaret could see the hope and excitement fading in his eyes as the colors fade from a drying seashell.

"Oh, Jo," she cried. "What are we going to *do?*"

"If we can't think of anything else we'll turn round, go back and hide again. Where's that bull you told me about?"

"Bull?" whispered Margaret.

"Yes. You said you were chased by a tethered bull at Splatt Bridge."

"We can't see him from here, if he's still where he was then. We might if we go further along the wood."

"Wait a moment. Let's watch them a little longer. It all depends whether they've seen us."

Margaret's heart was beginning to bounce with a new dread, the terror of her remembered nightmares. The palms of her hands were icy patches. To stop herself from thinking about the bull she screwed up her eyes and peered along the narrowing streak of water until the bridge seemed to dance and flicker. But between the flickerings, the tiny people appeared lounging and unexcited. There was a small flurry, and the litter tilted, but it was only a change of bearers.

"All right," said Jonathan. "Let's find your bull."

The children crept along the edge of the leafless wood, away from the canal; it was difficult not to walk on tiptoe.

"There he is," said Margaret.

Even at this distance the bull looked dangerous, tilted forward by the weight of his huge shoulders and bony head. The cruel horns were invisible, but Margaret knew their exact curve.

"No cows with him," said Jonathan. "He'll be in a real temper."

"What are you going to do?" whispered Margaret.

"I don't want to turn round and go back if we can help it," said Jonathan. "Some people must have seen us pass, even if they couldn't get out in time to try and stop us, so they'll probably be hunting down the canal after us. And even if we do get through, they'll probably stir up enough people to hunt us down in Gloucester. But if I can cut the bull's tether and bait him toward the bridge, he'll clear the men off for long enough for me to open the locking-pieces, and then you could simply barge the bridge open. They haven't brought horses. They won't catch us after that."

"You'll have to borrow Scrub. Caesar would be hopeless at that sort of thing."

"So would I. I'll do it on foot."

Margaret felt cold all over, a cold not from the bitter wind but spreading out from inside her. She knew Jonathan hadn't a chance of beating the bull on foot, any more than she had a chance of managing *Heartsease*. The plan was the wrong way around.

"I'd rather do the bull," she said. "I can ride Scrub. We'd both be better at our jobs that way. How do I cut the tether?"

Jonathan tilted his head sideways and looked at her until she turned away.

"It's the only hope," she said.

"Yes. It's better odds. And if it goes wrong at least you've a chance to get away. We'll try it like that. I found a carving knife in the ironmonger's in Gloucester—I liked it because it was so sharp—and if you can slash at the rope when the bull has pulled it taut you should be able to cut it in one go. *Heartsease* will make a tremendous cloud of smoke when she starts again, and they'll all be watching the canal after that. Then it will be six or seven minutes before I reach the bridge if I come down flat out. You'll have to time it from that, because you don't want to clear the bridge too early, or they'll simply dodge the bull and come back."

"What about Lucy and Tim?"

"I'll need Lucy to control the engine."

"Couldn't we cut a pole for Otto to do that with? Then Lucy and Tim and Caesar could come down after me, and get away if things go wrong. I'm going to ride down behind that long bank over there—it's called the Tumps on the map—so that I can't be seen from the bridge. If it all works, the men will be on the wrong side after the bridge is open, so we could wait for Lucy and Tim beyond it. If it doesn't, they might be able to escape."

"Um," said Jonathan. "I'll go and talk to them. And Otto. But I'll need Lucy to help me start the engines, so she won't be able to leave until you're almost in position—they'll be a long way behind you."

"Never mind," said Margaret. "At least it means Tim won't try to stop me teasing the bull."

Jonathan laughed.

"He doesn't look as if he needed much teasing," he said. "You move off while I show Lucy where to go. I'll give you twenty minutes before I start up."

"The knife," said Margaret.

"Yes, of course."

They went back to the boat. Lucy was sitting on the bulwark with her head in her hands; Tim was tickling Davey's stomach on the foredeck. Jonathan scampered aboard while Margaret looked over Scrub's harness and tightened the girth a notch. He came back with a knife which was almost like a scimitar, with a knobby bone handle made from the antler of a deer; she tried it with her thumb and found that it had the almost feathery touch of properly sharpened steel. Too scared to speak, she nodded to her cousin, raised her hand to Lucy and led Scrub away under the trees.

After a hundred yards they worked through a broken fence into an overgrown lane, with another small wood on their left; beyond that she turned south, still screened by trees, parallel with the canal but four hundred yards nearer the great river. At the far corner of the wood she found she could see neither Splatt Bridge nor the bull, so, hoping that meant that none of her enemies could see her either, she mounted and cantered on over the plashy turf. Scrub was still moving easily, his hooves squirting water sideways at every pace as he picked the firmest going between the dark green clumps of quill grass that grew where the ground was at its most spongy. Two furlongs, and their path was barred by a wide drainage ditch, steep-banked, the water in it flowing sluggishly toward the Severn. Scrub stretched his pace, gathered himself for the leap and swept across. Now they were riding along the far side of the Tumps.

This was a long, winding embankment, old and grassy, built (presumably) to stop the Severn from flooding in across Frampton long before the canal was dug. The map showed that it dipped sharply in toward Splatt Bridge. They reached the place far sooner than she wanted, but she dismounted at once and whispered to Scrub to stay where he was and taste the local grass. Then she wriggled to the top of the bank.

The bridge was three hundred yards away, straight ahead but half hidden by the patchy saplings of a neglected hedge. Much nearer, more to her right, stood the enemy of her dreams. The bull was already disturbed in his furious wits by the crowd on the bridge, and had strained to the limit of his tether in the hope of wreaking his anger and frustration on them. The best thing would be to snake through the grass and cut his tether while he fumed at Mr. Gordon and his cronies. Surely he wouldn't notice if she came from straight behind. There was plenty of time.

But she couldn't do it. To be caught there, helpless, too slow to escape the charging monster . . . She lay and sweated and swore at herself, but her limbs wouldn't take her over the bank.

Suddenly a savage cackling and hooting rose from the bridge. Through the bare branches of the hedge she could see arms pointing upstream. She looked that way herself. Clear above the distant wood rose a foul cloud of murk, that could have come only from some wicked engine.

She ran back to Scrub, mounted and trotted him along the bank until she thought they were opposite where the bull was tethered; then she nudged her heel into his ribs and he swept up over the bank, and down the far side. She'd been hoping to catch the bull while he was straining toward the shouting voices; but he must have heard the drub of hooves, for his head was already turned toward her and even as Scrub was changing feet to take the downward slope the horns lowered and the whole mass of beef and bone was flowing toward her as fast as cloud-shadow in a north wind. She could see from the circle of trampled grass how far his tether reached; she was safe outside it, but she could never cut the rope unless she took Scrub inside it.

Scrub saw the coming enemy and half shied away, but she forced his head around and touched his ribs again to tell him that she knew what she was up to. When the bull was so close that she could see the big eyes raging and the froth of fury around the nostrils, she jerked sideways at the precise moment in Scrub's stride which would whisk him to the right, and as the bull belted past she leaned forward to slash at the tautening rope.

The first slash missed completely, and the second made no more than a white nick in the gray hemp; then the enemy had turned.

The bull was dreadfully quick on his feet, considering how much he weighed; he seemed to flick his mass around and be flowing toward her before she had really balanced herself back into the saddle. But Scrub was still moving toward the center of the trampled circle, and even before she asked him he accelerated into a gallop. She knew he didn't like this game at all.

But he turned when she told him, out on the un-churned grass, and they tried again. It was a question of swaying out around the charge of the bull, allowing for the extra width of the sweep of his awful horns, and then at once swaying in to come closer to the rope than they had before. And this time she would have to lean backward, away from the pommel and stirrups of the sidesaddle. But Scrub's pace was all wrong, and she knew this before they reached the circle, so she took him wide out of range with several yards to spare. They halted on the far side of the circle and prepared for another pass. In the stillness between the two bouts of action she heard the men's voices again, deeper and more menacing than before. She glanced up the canal and saw the black funnel about three hundred yards away. It would have to be this time.

By now Scrub seemed to know what was wanted of him. As the eight hooves rushed the two animals together he swayed sideways at the last moment in a violent jerk, and then in again. Margaret couldn't tell whether she'd controlled him into this perfect movement, or whether he'd done it on his own, but there was the rope, taut as a bowstring, beside her knees. She stabbed the knife under it and hacked upward. The rope broke and the bull was free.

She flashed a glance over her shoulder; the bull had already turned and was coming at her again. Something about the way he held his head told her that he too knew that the rules of the game had changed. Now all that mattered was which of the two animals was faster. And where was the best gap in the ruined hedge.

There was no time to think. She saw a wide hole in the bushes a little to her left, just behind the bridge, so she nudged Scrub toward it. The men were making such a clamor now that she couldn't hear the hoofbeats of the bull. As she came through the gap she saw that her moment was exactly ripe: the men were on the bridge still, all their attention toward the tug which was booming down toward them with a solid wave under its bows; two of them had arrows ready, tense on the pulled strings; the rest had spears and billhooks. Above them all Mr. Gordon crouched in his swaying litter, his face purple, his fist raised to the bleak sky.

Margaret gave a shrieking yell, and two heads turned.

A mouth dropped open, an arm clutched at the elbow of one of the bowmen. More heads turned, and the color of the faces changed. Then, like reeds moving in a gust of wind, the whole group of bodies altered their stance—no longer straining toward the tug, but jostling in panic flight away from the bull. As Margaret reached the white railing that funneled in to the bridge, a half-gap opened in the crowd. She leaned over Scrub's neck, yelled again, and drove him through it. His shoulder slammed into the back of one of the litter bearers and she saw the crazy structure begin to topple, and heard, above all the clamor, a wild, croaking scream. Then she was over the bridge and wrenching him around to wait beside the canal while the rout of men fled down the lane and the bull thundered behind them.

She rushed Scrub back onto the bridge and leaped down by the crank. The wreck of the litter hung half over the railings and something was flopping in the water below her, but she hadn't time to look. She snapped the locks up and began to turn the handle. The bull was snorting in the middle of the lane while the men struggled through hedges. One man lay still in the middle of the road, and the legs of another wriggled in a thorny gap. She cranked on, and suddenly found that the handle would turn no more. The bridge was open, and pat on time *Heartsease* came churning through.

"Look out!" yelled Jonathan from the wheelhouse, pointing up the road.

She looked over her shoulder. The bull had turned. Beyond it two men with spears hesitated by gaps in the hedges. The bull snorted, shook its head, lowered its horns and was surging back toward her; and the men behind it were coming in her direction too.

"I'll wait for you," shouted Jonathan. Margaret swung onto Scrub's back and skipped him from the end of the bridge onto the little path that ran up beyond the deserted cottage where the bridgekeeper had lived. Forty yards further up, *Heartsease* was edging in to the bank, and by the time they reached it, was almost still; without orders Scrub picked his way over the bulwark and stood quivering where Caesar had been. Margaret slipped down and caressed the taut neck while the engine renewed its heavy boom and the smoke rose, puff-puff-puff, from the ridiculous funnel.

When Scrub had stopped quivering she walked along to the wheelhouse.

"Father was there," said Jonathan.

"I didn't see him."

"I think he got away all right."

"There was one man lying in the lane, but his trousers were the wrong color. And somebody fell into the water, I think."

"That was Mr. Gordon—I saw him topple. I wish Father hadn't come."

"Perhaps he was going to try and do what he could for us if we were caught."

"I hope so."

"How long must we wait for Tim and Lucy?"

"I'll pull in here. Marge, you were quite right—I couldn't have managed that, not possibly. Now I want to go and tell Otto what happened. Just watch the bridge, in case they get across while I'm below."

Splatt Bridge was half a mile astern now, looking almost as small as it had when they had first peered over the bank at the other end of the straight. Margaret tied the hawser to a sapling on the bank and then led Scrub ashore; the pony moved off a few yards and began to browse among the withered grasses, looking for blades with sap in them; then he found a small pool and drank. The bleak wind, scouring the fens and hissing through leafless thickets, seemed to be made of something harder than ordinary air, and colder too. Margaret crouched in the shelter of the wheelhouse and watched the men on the bridge.

They were bending at the rails, and at first Margaret thought they were trying to fathom the workings of the crank; but they moved, and she saw they were busy with something in the water.

A hoof clopped on stone; peeking around the wheelhouse she saw Lucy leading Caesar out of the meadow on their left, with Tim walking beside her.

"Did you kill him?" said Lucy, her voice almost a whisper.

"Who?"

"Mr. Gordon. I saw him fall in."

"Ah, please God no!" cried Margaret. Lucy smiled at her—the same smile as she sometimes watched Tim with.

"Aye," she said. "Best dead, but not when one of us has to be killing him. Shall we be sailing on now?"

"As soon as possible, I think," said Margaret.

But nothing would make Caesar go aboard the tug again, not though Scrub stepped daintily on and off a dozen times. After Jonathan had tugged and bullied, after Margaret had flattered and coaxed, they decided to leave him.

"Perhaps he'll follow us," said Jonathan.

"Perhaps," said Margaret. "Anyway the winter's over, and he'll be all right. Nothing the weather can do can hurt a pony—that's what the old stableboy told me."

"Only four more bridges," said Jonathan with a slight change of voice which made Margaret realize that he'd only been pretending to worry about Caesar to keep *her* happy—left to himself he'd have abandoned his pony long before.

"One of them's in Purton," said Margaret, "and there's people living there."

"Two on the map," said Jonathan.

"I only remember one."

"Well, you'd best get right ahead and scout. It's four miles yet, and round a bend. If we have to, we'll stop the engine and let Scrub tow us through."

"Do you think they'd allow us to open the bridges if we told them our story?"

"Let's hope."

Heartsease, as if in triumph over the battle of Splatt Bridge, spouted her largest and nastiest plume of smoke when she restarted. Scrub cantered easily down the towpath, quite rested from his battle with the bull. The first gate moved like the others, but the second, in the middle of a huge emptiness with only the white spire of Slimbridge Church to notch the horizon, was stuck. In the end Jonathan had to ram it open, backing *Heartsease* off and charging a dozen times with fenders over the bow before something in the structure gave way with a sharp crack. Then Tim and she together just managed to wind the opening section around so that the tug could go through. It seemed too much work to shut it again, so Jonathan ferried them across to the towpath.

"I didn't enjoy that at all," he said. "Purton's about two miles on now. You get well ahead and see what's best, and I'll wait half a mile out until you come back—if I've got the contours right there's a little hill which will screen us."

So there was a long, easy canter, dead level, with Scrub's hooves knocking out the rhythm of rapid travel. The estuary gleamed wide on her right, at about half-tide—so if it was ebbing they'd have a dangerously long nine hours to wait before high tide, and if it was flooding they'd have a bare three. Three seemed nothing like enough to be sure of finding out how the lock worked, but quite long enough for angry men to come swarming after them.

Scrub suddenly became bored with hurrying when they were almost at the last bend and slowed to a shambling walk, so Margaret dismounted and led him along the towpath. She'd have liked to leave him to rest and browse while she went on alone to explore, but she hadn't quite the courage to go among dangerous strangers without her means of escape—Scrub could gallop faster than the angriest man in England could run. The first bridge was open, which was why she hadn't remembered it, but the second was shut. Worse still, a fishing rod was lashed to the further railings, its float motionless on the gray water, and that meant that someone must be watching the bridge. But at least the locking-bar on her end was open. She led Scrub across, peering over hedges on either side of the street.

He was in the garden of the first house on the right, a fat lump of a man lying almost on his back in a cane chair, wrapped in blankets and coats against the bitter wind. A straw hat covered most of his face, so that Margaret couldn't tell whether he was watching the float through a gap in his fence, or listening for the bell at the end of the rod, or sleeping.

"Good morning," she called—softly, so as not to break his precious sleep, if he was asleep.

The hat was brushed back by a mottled hand, and an angry blue eye peered at her from above a purple cheekbone, but he said nothing.

"You're a long way from your rod," said Margaret cheerfully.

"Three seconds," the man grunted, and shoved his hat forward.

Margaret felt sick. He was much too big and much too close—it took forty seconds to open a bridge, even if it moved easily. She walked back over the bridge but stopped close by the handle.

"Lame?" she said, as if she was talking to a baby. "Oh, you are a big softy—let me have a look. Why, it's only a tiny pebble. There, that's better, isn't it?"

Scrub was not a good actor; anyone actually watching could have seen how puzzled he was to have a perfectly sound hoof lifted up, peered into, poked at and put down again. While she was kneeling Margaret flipped the locking piece of the bridge over, and as she rose she gave the handle a single turn, trusting the fidgeting hooves to drown the noise, to see whether it would move at all. It did, and at the far end she could see the crack in the film of dried mud which showed where the join had begun to part. Then she mounted and rode slowly up the canal and told Jonathan what she had seen and done.

"Three seconds is useless," he said. "We'll have to lure him away. Are there a lot of other people in the village?"

"I didn't see any, but I think there must be—all the gardens are dug and weeded."

"Probably they're having dinner. If you rode back in a frenzy and said there was something wicked coming down the canal but you could only see it properly from the other bridge, he'd run up there and you'd have time to get that bridge open. If you time it right, you could point to the smoke."

"I'll try," said Margaret, though she didn't feel from the look of the fat fisher's eye that he would be an easy man to lie to. She cantered back reining Scrub in every few paces and then letting him go again so that he would seem properly fretful when they reached the village. She rehearsed cries—was "Help!" a better beginning or "Please . . ."?

No need. The rod was there, but the fat man was gone from his garden.

She jumped down and started to wind frenziedly at the handle. The end of the bridge had moved a yard when there was a shout behind her and something flicked past her ear, banged on the railing and dropped into the water; she looked around—he was behind the fence, his hand raised to throw another stone. She gave a meaningless shout and, still cranking, pointed with her free hand to the space between rooftops where the familiar black puffs rose before they were scattered by the wind. He wheeled around, stared, ran to the far hedge, stared again, and bellowed. Windows in the village opened with bangs or squeaks.

"Oi, you girl, you lay off!" he shouted. "We'll catch un here!"

Nearly far enough. Margaret cranked on. Pain blazed into her left shoulder. She gave the handle five more turns, dodged sideways and heard the splash of a stone, turned thrice more and ran to where Scrub waited out on the arm of the swinging bridge. Her shoulder was still fiery with pain when she twisted up into the saddle and urged him forward. A stone grazed his quarters and rapped her heel. Startled, he gathered himself and sprang straight out over the waiting water. There was a roaring splash, freezing water blinding her eyes, burning her nostrils, panic. But she'd remembered to lean right forward, and kept her seat as Scrub's body tilted into its swimming posture. The roaring died, though the deadly cold remained, and they were swimming slantways toward the far bank with Scrub's head and her own head and shoulders rising above the water but the rest of them covered from the old man's stones. Then she heard shouts behind, and a tinkle of breaking glass. They'd stopped throwing at *her*.

She looked back up the canal and saw half a dozen men bending and flinging as *Heartsease* surged around the curve, but they were too lost in the rage and drama of action to think of crowding onto the open bridge, from which they could have boarded as the tug went past. She was still watching the fight when something tickled her neck—a blade of grass. Scrub had reached the bank, but it was too steep for him to climb. She scrambled soddenly up, and with her weight off him he managed it. But she knew she would die of cold in ten minutes unless she could find something dry to wear.

Jonathan must have known it too, for he was already slowing the tug as he came abreast of her.

"Dry clothes in the cabin!" he shouted through a smashed window, his face streaming with blood.

"Are you all right?" she called back, in the accents of a fussing mum.

"Only bits of glass. Doesn't hurt. Get aboard."

The stove was still going in the cabin, and the close air warm as a drying cupboard. Margaret stripped and rummaged through a big cardboard box full of clothing. Jonathan must have raided a department store for Lucy. She dried herself on a blanket and then put on a vest, two pairs of jeans and two thick jerseys—it didn't seem the time for the tempting little frocks. Then she started to hang out her own sodden clothes to dry over the stove, but there wasn't room, so she took them all off the line again and rolled them into a tight bundle tied with her belt. She took the blanket up to rub down Scrub.

They were already far down the last arm of the canal, where it ran tight against the river with only a thirty-yard-wide embankment to separate its listless waters from the rushing tides of the Severn. Only when the pony was nearly dry did she remember about Jonathan's face.

His left eye was glued shut with drying blood, and his lip swollen to a blue bubble, but he hummed to himself as he stood at the large wheel, twitching it occasionally to keep the tug dead in the center of the canal. The main cut in his forehead had stopped flowing, and he said nothing while Margaret sponged and dabbed. She found he wasn't as injured as he'd looked, and the moment she stopped worrying about him she felt the pain nagging again at her own shoulder. He must have noticed the sudden tightening of her movements.

"Did he hit you?" he said. "He looked too close to miss."

At once she was ashamed.

"Only one stone," she said. "It just hurts when I think about it."

"You've got us through twice now," he said. "I was an idiot second time; and an idiot to let Caesar go, too. He could have towed us through."

"I don't think they'd have allowed us to open the bridge anyway."

"I didn't think about towing till too late—you get in a mood when you're just going to blind through, and you don't *want* to stop to think. They're right about machines, somehow—Mr. Gordon and his lot, I mean. Machines eat your mind up until you think they're the answer to everything. I noticed it that morning when you stopped Mr. Gordon hypnotizing Mother; all I could think of was some sort of *contrivance,* and there wasn't one."

"Lucy says I killed Mr. Gordon," said Margaret.

"No you didn't!" said Jonathan hotly. "I saw his litter keel over and tip him in, and I didn't see him climb out. But if he's dead, he killed himself. Something like this was going to happen, for sure. He'd have pushed some-body too far—somebody like Father with a mind of his own—and they'd have gone for him with a billhook."

"Yes," said Margaret. "But it was me."

She stared through the shattered windows at the wide, drear landscape. It was so different from the hills because, though you could see just as much of the scur-rying and steely sky, you couldn't see more than a few furlongs of earth. The land lay so flat that distances lost meaning—even the mile-wide Severn on their right looked only a grim band of water between the muddy band of bank in the foreground and the reddish band of cliffs beyond. And the hills of home, the true hills, the Cotswolds, might just as well have been clouds on the left horizon, so unreachable seemed the distance to them.

"Lord, that's a big tower!" said Jonathan. He pointed ahead to where the warehouse at Sharpness soared out of the flatness, less than a mile away.

"High tide just under three hours," he added. "Otto worked it out from old tide tables—it's time we got him on deck. Could you ask Lucy to persuade Tim? And there's a dustpan and brush in the cabin, if you felt like getting rid of this broken glass."

Scrub was standing in the oval of space behind the engine room roof, watching with mild boredom as the bank slid past. Margaret knelt at the engine room hatch; the torrid air, blasting through the small opening, smelled of wicked things: burned fuel, reeking oil and metal fierce with friction. Each cylinder stamped out its separate thud above the clanging and hissing. Otto lay in his corner, watching Lucy and the signal dial. She stood by the control lever and watched it too, frowning. Tim slept in the middle of the racket, crouched in a gangway like a drowsing ape, with Davey asleep in his arms. Margaret hated the idea of going down, so she yelled and yelled again. Lucy glanced up. The oily face smiled, and said something, and an oily hand gestured at the dial. Margaret nodded, beckoned and pointed forward. Lucy shrugged and left her post.

"Sorry," said Margaret as her head poked out of the hatch. "Jo wants Tim to bring Otto on deck."

Lucy nodded and stared across the choppy estuary.

"Shouldn't fancy living in these parts," she said. "I'll wake Tim."

Margaret found the dustpan and brush and swept out the wheelhouse. When she threw the last splinters overboard she saw that they'd finished with hedges and fields and were moving between sidings and timber yards; and *Heartsease* was going much more slowly too.

"Are the bridges the same as the others?" called Jonathan. "One's got a railway on it. You'll have to land and open them."

"There's one high one, but I don't remember the other," said Margaret.

"Funny. . . . Anyway, there's the high one—we can get under that. And there's the other, and it's open. Lord, that *is* a big tower!"

The huge, windowless column of concrete on the south side of the dock came nearer and nearer. The

canal widened as it curved. Around the corner lay the
big ship which had so astonished Margaret; *Heartsease*
seemed like a dinghy beside it. Then, right across the
water, ran a low, dark line with a frill of railing above it
in one place. The line was the quay at the bottom of the
docks, and the frill was the guardrails for the narrow
footpath on top of the lock gates. It was here the canal
ended—and their escape, too, if they couldn't find how
to open the lock gates.

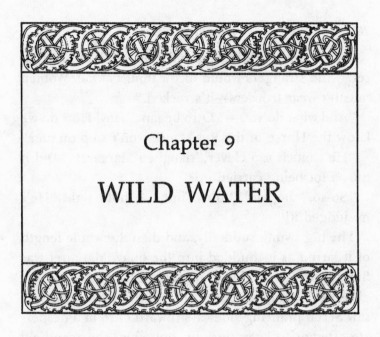

Chapter 9

WILD WATER

Otto lay out on deck beside Scrub, as pale as plaster with his illness and long hiding from daylight. Tim knelt by him, bubbling worriedly—and Margaret thought that the paleness might also be pain, the pain of being heaved with ribs half mended up a vertical iron ladder. But he smiled wickedly at her as she walked aft.

"Hi, Heroine of the Resistance," he said. "I sure wish I'd taken a movie of you playing your bull, just to show the folks back home. You look like a girl back home, too, in that rig. Nice."

Margaret felt herself flush, and glanced down at her primrose-yellow jersey and scarlet jeans. They made her feel like someone else.

"Pity your own folk can't see you," said Otto.

"Uncle Peter would whip me if he did," said Margaret. "And strangers would throw things at me. Women mustn't wear trousers—it's wicked."

"And what do you—" Otto began. "Hey! How do we know the Horse of the Resistance won't step on me?"

"He's much too clever," laughed Margaret. "Did it hurt a lot being carried up?"

"So-so," he said, "but Tim . . . hold tight! He's misjudged it!"

The tug swung suddenly, and then the whole length of it jarred as it thudded into the quay. Margaret was flung to the deck, almost putting her arm through the glass of the engine room roof. As she went down she saw Scrub prancing sideways toward Otto in a desperate attempt to keep upright; but when she rose he'd stopped, with his forelegs actually astride the sick man. Delicately he moved himself away.

"I told you he was clever," said Margaret with a shudder.

"Sorry!" called Jonathan from the wheelhouse. "I made a mess of that. Is Lucy all right?"

"Fair enough," answered Lucy, poking her head through the hatch. "I burned my arm on that engine of yours, but not enough to notice."

"Margaret can put some cream on it," said Jonathan. "In the first-aid bag in the cabin, Marge. But first, Lucy, can you get Tim to carry Otto ashore to look at the sluices?"

Tim thought it was an unwise move. Margaret was astonished by how much you could tell from the tone of his bubbling and the way he moved his head; now he was arguing that his patient had been under quite enough of a strain coming up from the engine room, and must rest before he attempted anything else. He began to back away as Lucy talked softly to him.

"Ah, come on, Tim, my old pal," said Otto suddenly. "I can stand it if you can."

Tim stopped backing away and knelt beside him, making little worried noises.

"Ah, come on," said Otto gently. "Jo's been stoned, Marge has fought a mad bull, Lucy's kept that engine going all morning—why can't I earn my medal too?"

Tim slithered an arm beneath his shoulders and another beneath his thighs and picked him up tenderly. He must have been very light with illness, as light as a dry bone. Margaret took Lucy below to dress her burn, which was a nasty patch of dead whiteness surrounded by angry red on the inside of her left forearm. There were aspirins, too, in the bag—Jonathan must have raided half the shops in Gloucester. Lucy grimaced as she chewed them up.

"D'you think I'm doing right, Miss Margaret?" said Lucy.

"How?"

"Taking Tim to America. Otto doesn't think they can make him *clever,* not like you nor me, but they might find drugs for him which'd make him two parts well; and Otto's uncle has a farm where we can live, he says. But what frights me is they might take Tim away and shut him up with a lot of other zanies—they wouldn't do that, would they?"

"Not if Otto says they won't. He owes you a lot—both of you."

"Aye," sighed Lucy. "But will they listen to him?"

"I wish I weren't going," said Margaret. "I wish none of this had ever happened. It's awful knowing nothing can ever be smooth and easy again."

Lucy grinned—not her usual secret smile but a real grin.

"I reckon we got no choice," she said. "Neither you nor me. Master Jonathan blows us along like feathers in the breeze. Let's look what he's at now."

Jonathan was down a deep hole in the quayside; the hole had a lid, which they'd opened, and Otto was propped on the rusting lip of iron which surrounded it.

"It's hydraulic," called Otto, "so there must be some kind of cylinder with a piston in it and a shaft. Then the shaft might thrust down on an arm and the other end of that might haul the sluice up. They'd be sure to have fixed it so you could haul it up by hand, in case the hydraulics failed. See anything?"

"I've got the main cylinder," said Jonathan as matter-of-factly as if he were talking about laying the supper table. "But the rest of it's not . . . oh, I see. How far would the sluice travel, do you think?"

"Four, five feet, I guess. Could be only two or three, if it's broad enough."

"That's it, then. There's two rings which'd take a

hook, one to shut and one to open. I can't begin to shift it, though."

"Don't try," called Otto urgently. "Fetch out that block and tackle you looted from the garage. We'll put a beam across."

Jonathan popped out of the hole and began scampering to the tug. All he'd done since yesterday evening didn't seem to have slowed him down at all.

"Come and help, Marge," he called as he disappeared down the cabin hatch.

By the time she got there he was handing up a thing which didn't look any use at all, made of two hooks and two pulley wheels and a great tangle of rusty chain. Margaret struggled with the heavy and awkward mess of metal back to where Otto lay, while Jonathan rabbited down into the engine room.

"Is there more of it?" she asked Otto.

"No, that's all. It ought to do the trick—got a twenty-to-one ratio, just about."

"Then we've still got to find something strong to lift it—Scrub could pull, I suppose."

"No need," he said, grinning. "See where the chains run over that top wheel? That pulley's double, and one side of it's a mite smaller than the other, so when the pulley goes round the loop in the middle, that bit there which the other pulley hangs from gets slowly bigger or smaller. But you've got to pull the chain outside the pulley a good yard to make the loop a couple of inches smaller, so you're pulling about twenty times as hard. You can lift twenty times your own weight. Got it?"

"No," said Margaret.

"You'll see," said Otto. "What's the gas for, Jo?"

Jonathan was bending beneath the weight of two big cans, just the same shape and size as the one he'd used to scatter petrol over the stones the night the whole fearful adventure began.

"Gas?" he said, putting them down. "It's petrol. Marge, will you and Lucy take a can each up to where the timber piles are thickest; there'll be men hunting us down from Purton soon. I saw a boat on the canal up there, so I think they'll cross and come down the tow-path. Pull a lot of planks out across the path, spray the petrol about, stand back and throw a lit rag on to it. Take rags and matches. Then go and do the same thing on the road the other side of the sheds—there's more timber beyond it, and if you can get it really blazing they'll never get through. I may have to harness Scrub to the capstan to open the gates—d'you think he'll do it for me if you aren't back?"

"Oh, yes," said Margaret. "How much have you got to do?"

"Shut the bottom sluice, open the top one, open the top gate when the water's level—it's only got about four foot to come up because the tide's high in the basin—put *Heartsease* in the lock, shut the top gate, shut the top sluice, open the bottom one, let the water go down again, open the bottom gate and we're out. Hurry up, though—I can't move *Heartsease* without Lucy in the engine room."

The girls trudged up beside the dock, straining sideways under the twenty-pound weight of the petrol cans. The wind bit at the backs of their necks and fingered icily through their clothes in spite of the exercise.

"Fine breeze for a bonfire," whispered Lucy.

Margaret did most of the timber hauling, but she didn't mind because Lucy seemed happy to handle the petrol. It was hard work, but quick once she'd found a stack of planks light enough for her to run out across the quay in a single movement. At the back of the shed the road and railway ran side by side, making a forty-foot gap before the further sheds. The girls toiled away, one on each side of the road, hauling out planks to make a barrier of fire, until Margaret saw that they were going about the job in an un-Jonathan-like way.

"That's enough," she said. "We'll never be able to pull out so much that there's fire right across the road. But if the sheds really catch it'll be too hot to get through."

"Right," said Lucy. "Shall I start this end, then? Wind's going round a bit, I fancy. Ugh! Wicked stuff, this petrol. You stand back, Miss Margaret, while I see what I can do with it."

She soaked several rags, scattered half of one can all over Margaret's pile and the wood beside it in the stack, then the other half over her own. In the shelter of the stacks the harsh wind eddied, blowing the weird reek about them. Lucy tied a stone into a soaked rag so clumsily that Margaret was sure it would fall out. She lit it and threw.

Half a second's hesitation, and with a bellowing sigh

the spread petrol exploded. In ten seconds the pile was blazing like a hayrick, huge sparks spiraling upward in the draft. One of these must have fallen into the second pile, for it exploded while Lucy was still tying another stone into a rag. Margaret picked up the other can and ran between the stacked planks to the quayside. Already they could hear the coarse roar of fire eating into the piled hills of old pine, dry with five summers, sheltered by the shed roofs from five winters. By the dock Lucy splashed the petrol about as though she were watering a greenhouse. The wind, still shifting around toward the northeast, smothered them with an eddy of smoke from the first fire, and in the gap that followed it Margaret thought she saw through her choking tears a movement far up the canal—a troop of men marching down the towpath; but the same booming whoosh of fire blotted out land and water.

The flames at the far end of the shed were already higher than the roof. Smoke piled skyward like a storm cloud. Timber stacks which they hadn't even touched were alight in a dozen places. Heat poured toward them on the wind, like a flatiron held close to the cheek. They ran back to the lock. The gates at the top were open.

"I thought I saw men coming down the towpath," gasped Margaret.

"Me too," said Lucy. "Nigh on a score of them."

"They won't get through that lot," said Jonathan, nodding toward the inferno of the timber yard. "Lucy, will you go and be engineer while we get her into the lock? Marge, as soon as she's in will you make Scrub haul on that capstan bar to close the gate? Otto and Tim might as well wait here."

As the tug nosed through the narrow gap left by the single gate being opened, Margaret studied her next job. The capstan was really a large iron cogwheel in a hole in the ground, protected by an iron lid which Jonathan had opened; below it lay inexplicable machinery; from the cog a stout wooden bar about seven feet long stuck out sideways, shaped so that it rose just clear of the rim of the hole. Scrub was harnessed on awkwardly short traces to the end of this pole: if he pulled hard enough, the cog would turn.

Margaret patted his neck and said, "Come on, boy." He hated horsecollars but was sensible enough to know that he had to endure them sometimes, so he leaned into the collar, hesitated when he found that the weight behind him was more than he was used to, then flung himself forward. With tiny, labored steps he moved over the cobbles; the moment the gate began to move, its slow momentum made the strain less; Margaret led him round and round, talking to him, telling him how strong and clever he was, but looking all the time over her shoulder to make sure they were pulling at right angles to the capstan bar.

At last Otto gave a shout, and she eased the pony off and untied the rope from the capstan. Jonathan was already down the sluice hole, hauling at a clacking chain which ran over the double pulley. Margaret leaned over and saw the lower hook gradually inching upward, but she still didn't understand how it worked.

"Strong hoss," said Otto, as she led Scrub toward the lower capstan.

"I don't know if he can do two more," said Margaret. "It's a horrid strain, and he always gets bored with that sort of thing rather quickly."

"Only one more, I hope," said Otto. "The gates out into the river, on the other side of the basin, they float open as the tide comes in. They're open now, see?"

And they were, too. That made the escape seem easier. Jonathan scurried past with his chains and pulleys, and Tim followed with the squat baulk of timber from which the pulleys were to hang. Davey came last of all, grabbing frivolously at Tim's heels. The flames gnawed into the timber with a noise like surf among reefs, and a rattling crackle told them that another stack had caught. In the shifting wind long orange tongues of fire flowed clean across the dock, reflected dully by the dull water. Jonathan worked his magic with the block and tackle and the lower sluice. *Heartsease* disappeared down into the lock, until only the top half of the funnel, the windows of the wheelhouse and a few feet of stubby mast were showing. Then she stopped—the lock water was level with the basin.

But this time Scrub couldn't move the capstan, for all Margaret's praise and coaxing. Lucy came up from the engine room to watch; then Jonathan said "Rest him a moment" and ran across the quay to a low office building, on whose side were arranged three shaped pieces of wood, each on its separate pair of hooks. He came back with them and fitted their square ends into the holes in the top of the capstan: they were the other capstan bars, by which the locks had been worked before the Changes if ever the power failed. He led Tim up to one bar, and showed him how to push. He and Lucy strained their backs against the other two, and Margaret led Scrub forward, watching the group around the capstan over her shoulder. Nothing moved.

"Come on, Tim," gasped Jonathan. "Push, Tim. Push hard. Like this."

Tim gazed at him, slack-jawed, bubbling. Then he leaned his broad shoulders against the bar and heaved, and they all fell to the ground together as the capstan turned. Jonathan was on his feet in a moment, but Lucy lay where she was, rubbing her head and looking sulkily across to where Otto lay laughing on the quayside.

"It's all right for some," she hissed, but Otto only laughed the more, while Scrub and Margaret circled slowly around, easing the gate open.

On the other side of the dock a petrol dump exploded like a bomb. Then the wind shifted right around to the true northeast and they were all coughing and weeping in the reeking smoke, dodging desperately toward what looked like clear patches but were only thinner areas of smoke where you still couldn't breathe, and then another onset of fume and darkness rushed down and overwhelmed them. In the middle of it all Scrub, still harnessed to the capstan, panicked. He pranced about the quay trying to rush away from the choking enemy and always being halted with a tearing jerk at the

end of the short rope. He was too crazed to notice
where his hooves were landing.

"Get down and crawl!" yelled Otto from the ground.
"It's okay down here! Crawl to the boat!"

Margaret dropped. He was right. Under the rushing
clouds there was a narrow seam of air which could still
be breathed, if she chose her moment. In it she could
see Jonathan already crawling toward the lock, and
Lucy crouching low and trying to drag Tim down. The
zany bent at last, then dropped on all fours and immediately scampered with a rapid baboon-like run toward
Otto. Otto spoke to him, but Margaret couldn't hear
what he said.

She never saw how Tim carried him to the boat, either, for suddenly an eddy of air pushed all the smoke
aside so that she could see Scrub, mad with terror of
burning, wallowing at the end of his rope. At once she
was on her feet. For several seconds Scrub didn't know
her and she could do nothing but hold his bridle and
dodge the flailing hooves. Then, as she crooned mean-
inglessly to him, like Tim talking to a sick beast, he
found a tiny island of trust in his mind, steadied and
stood still. Before the smoke overwhelmed them again
she managed to back him to a point where she could
loose him from the traces, her fingers moving so fast
among the straps and buckles that she didn't have to tell
them what to do. As the horrible smoke swept over
them she took hold of the bridle and forced Scrub's
head down toward the cobbles; bending double she
scuttered toward the lock. He saw the patch of calm and

smokeless air below him and skipped delicately down to the deck, where he stood snorting and shivering.

"Ship's crew mustered!" cried Otto. "Horse and all! We're away!"

The big engine boomed. The water churned in the lock and the quay slid backward. Then they were out in the wide acre of the tidal basin, with the smoke streaming past a foot or two above their heads. Only the far gates now, and they'd escaped.

But the gates were shut. For the first time Margaret saw Otto look worried.

"Tide must have started to ebb and sucked 'em in," he said. "They were open quarter of an hour back, weren't they, Marge?"

"Couldn't we pull them open?" called Jonathan from the wheelhouse. "If we got a hawser up there quickly."

"Worth a go," said Otto.

"I'll take it up," said Margaret. "It'll take longer if you do it, Jo. Lucy, make Tim look after Scrub, or he'll think I'm leaving him."

It was an awkward six-foot scramble, up a rusty projection which supported a screw-topped bar; the heavy hawser tugged at her belt. She had to lie flat on her face on the catwalk at the top of the gate to fasten the hawser to a stanchion below her—the rails on either side of the catwalk didn't look strong enough. Panting, she backed off the top of the gate onto the quay, trying to work out how much the tide had fallen since the gates had closed —barely a couple of inches, she thought. She watched anxiously as the slack of the hawser rose dripping from

the basin, became a shallow curve, became a stiff line.
Jonathan put his signal lever over and the water under
the stern erupted into boiling foam. The bows came up.
The rope groaned. The gate moved an inch, three
inches, and Margaret could see the creased lines at the
gap where the water hunched and poured through.
Then everything altered as the gate swung past the
pressure line. *Heartsease* backed off with a jerk like a
rearing pony and the gate swung fully open with the
basin water tearing through. The hawser snapped like
wool, but with a deep twang, as the tug reached the end
of its tether; but Margaret had already grasped the
spare length of hawser which she'd left beyond the
place she'd tied it (Jonathan's suggestion, of course)
and before the gate could swing shut she'd taken three
turns around a bollard on the shore.

The fierce haul of the engine dragged the tug out
toward the middle of the basin before Jonathan could
halt it and make for the gap again. He headed slowly in,
anxious not to spoil his victory at the last minute by
charging into the wall or the other gate. The smoke was
thinner here, but still rushing past in choking and tear-
producing swirls. As Margaret crouched under it, waiting, she heard a hoarse cry. She hopped around, still
crouching, and saw a big man galloping toward her
through the murk with an ax swung up over his shoulder. He was thirty yards off, but he'd seen her—it was
her he was coming for. She scrambled through the two
sets of railings on top of the gate, hung for an instant to
a stanchion as she leaned out and tensed herself, then

leaped for the nearing bows of *Heartsease*. The world
reeled and hurtled, and the bulwarks slammed into her
knees and she was turning head over heels on the rough
iron of the deck. Her ear must have hit something, for it
was singing as she started to heave herself up. The ax
clanged onto the iron two feet in front of her face,
bounced and rocketed overboard. The man was trying
to follow it, but *Heartsease* was through the gap before
he could disentangle himself from the double railings.
He stood and shook his fist, gigantic amid the smoke.
Margaret, her head still ringing, walked aft.

"I saw him coming before you did," said Jonathan
through the broken window. "Tell you later—Otto says
I must shave this breakwater close as I can."

They were racing along beside a strange structure of
huge beams, all green with seaweed, which stretched
out into the estuary. There was another on the far side
of the harbor entrance, curving away upriver, and between the two breakwaters the river surface was level
and easy; but out beyond them Margaret could see the
full Severn tide foaming seaward. She thought Jonathan had misjudged his course, that they were going to
ram one of the enormous beams right on the corner,
but it whisked by barely a yard from the bulwarks. She
wanted to lean out and touch it—the last morsel of
England, maybe, that she would ever feel—but it was
too far for safety.

Then the whole boat heeled sideways for an instant
as the racing waters gripped it, before Jonathan turned
the bow downstream and they were moving toward Ire-

land with the combined speed of a six-knot tide and a ten-knot engine. Margaret looked aft to where the streaming pother of smoke was marked at the actual places where the wood was burning by the orange glow of house-high flames. Just as she was thinking how fast they were moving away from that hideous arena she saw Scrub skitter sideways as the boat lurched in the tide race. He almost went overboard. She ran back to him, staggering along the gangway, took his bridle and tried to gentle and calm him while he found his sea legs. Soon he was standing much more steadily, his legs splayed out and braced, so she tied his reins to a shackle just aft of the engine room roof and poured out a little hill of corn for him to nose at.

That made her realize how hungry she was. She walked forward to where Otto lay on the raised bit of deck in front of the wheelhouse; he had his chart spread out beside him, and Tim had propped him on a rolled tarpaulin so that he could watch the far shore and try to pick out the landmarks which would steer them down the twisting and treacherous channel.

"When's dinner?" she said.

"Just about as soon as you've got it ready, Marge. You're cook, because Lucy can't leave the engine and Jo and I must get this hulk ten miles downriver before the tide goes out. This is some cranky bit of water, and I don't like the feel of the wind, neither."

Margaret looked at the sky. Now that they were out from under the pother of smoke she could see that it had indeed changed. All morning it had seemed like a neutral gray roof over the bleak flats—it had been the wind that hurt, but the sky had seemed harmless. Now, to the northeast, it had darkened like a bruise. The wind must have risen, too, for it seemed no less and they were moving with it at fifteen knots. The waves, even in these narrow waters, seemed to be growing bigger. She looked anxiously aft to where Scrub was feeding in snatches as the deck bucketed beneath him.

"Easy!" shouted Otto. "There's Berkeley—three points right, Jo, to round Black Rock. If you can spot the line of the current, steer a mite outside it on the way out, then inside it on the way in."

"I can see two buoys still there," called Jonathan.

"Lift me up, Marge," said Otto. "Manage? Fine. Outside both of 'em, Jo, then sharp back inshore. Marge, food!"

She opened cans in the cabin and spooned chilly messes of stew into the plastic mugs which Jonathan had stolen—but the spoons were elegant, stainless steel with black handles, marked MADE IN SWEDEN. The crew took their helpings without a word, and began at once to eat with one hand while they did their work with the other—except Tim, who fed himself and Davey with alternate spoonfuls. It would have been a horrid meal if they hadn't all been hungry enough to eat anything. She found a bucket for Scrub and half filled it with the nasty water of the canal from one of the big oil drums; she had to hold it up under his nose while he drank, because the boat was fidgeting too much in the churning tide for it to stand safe on the deck. When she'd finished she looked around again and saw that Jonathan had steered them right out to the far shore of the estuary, and they were now heading back toward England under the gigantic tracery of the Severn Bridge. The blackness from the north was covering half the sky and there were feathers of snow in the wind. Tim had come on deck and was trying to coax Otto below, but Otto just grinned at him and shook his head, so Tim clambered down into the cabin and returned with a great bundle of blankets which he spread around his patient; Otto allowed himself to be babied, but all the time he was watching the shore and glancing down at his flapping chart.

As Margaret was collecting the empty mugs the first real wave came washing along the scuppers, knee-deep and foaming. She had just time to fling herself up to the stretch of higher deck between the wheelhouse and the engine room roof as it ran sucking past; she lay panting on the tilted iron. As she rose Jonathan opened the wheelhouse door with a hand behind his back.

"Shut the engine room hatch as you go past," he shouted, still peering forward. "And for the Lord's sake hang on tight. I can't turn to pick you up in this."

He shut the door before she could tell him how furious she was at his having swept them all into this stupid adventure, so she clawed aft, holding on to anything holdable. The engine room was the same oil-smelling, clamorous hole, but now she couldn't really hear how noisy it was because the wind and the waves were making such a hissing and smashing that anywhere out of their power seemed quiet. She shouted down to Lucy that she was closing the hatch. Lucy must have heard her voice but not the actual words, because she looked up inquiringly. Margaret made signals; the tired face nodded; Margaret shut her in.

Scrub must have fallen once—there was a slight bleeding from his knee—but he was on his feet now, legs spread wider than ever. The waves rinsed down the scuppers and out of the ports on either side, sometimes washing right over his hooves as he braced himself on the reeling deck. No human can know what a horse really thinks. They have a memory, certainly, for a hunter will often find his way home unerringly across country which he hasn't seen for a year or more; but their idea of before and after must be different from ours, weaker, less useful; *now* is what matters. And *now*, for Scrub, was a rusty, clanging platform which reeled from side to side, and beyond it dangerous frothing water, such as never ran in any river a horse could drink from; no turf, no trees, no stables, only a senseless whirling universe which he couldn't escape from because he was tied to a shackle in the middle of the deck. He was on the edge of madness when Margaret stroked his desperate neck and spoke to him.

She stood there for almost an hour, watching the storming estuary and the muddle of charging clouds, and trying to guess which way the deck would next cant, so that she could help him prepare for the new posture. Snow whirled and stung. Sometimes she could barely see fifty yards from the boat, but then there would come a space between squalls, and land loomed in sight on their left, less than half a mile away, wheeling backward. The waves were not ordered; they came at *Heartsease* in all shapes and from all directions, with none of the ranked inevitability of midocean—the only inevitable thing was that they became steadily larger. And the sky became blacker. It would soon be night.

But there was still a long stretch of this rough ocean to cover, and poor Scrub was still burdened with all his harness, including the heavy horsecollar and the ponderous sidesaddle—no point in either of them any longer. She loosed the reins from the shackle and, talking to steady him all the time, lifted the collar over his head and laid it down on the deck.

A roar like cannon split their closed world, and a single bolt of lightning turned boat and sea and sky into a blinding whiteness which printed itself on her retinas through closed eyelids. Scrub shied toward the bulwarks, and at the same moment the tug (Jonathan must have been startled enough to let the wheel go) swung sideways onto the waves. One big hill of water heaved across the deck and smothered her, bashing her into knobs and surfaces of iron until it pinned her to the bulwark and poured away. She lay and gasped for an instant, then wrenched herself onto hands and knees to see what had become of Scrub.

He was overboard.

She cried aloud as she saw his neck and shoulders spear up above a wave, slip into a trough and rise again. He was trying to follow the boat, to follow her.

"Stop! Stop!" she yelled, but already the shape of the water under the stern was different as Jonathan backed perilously up into the following seas. But there was no hope of hauling the pony aboard, not even with Tim to help, no way for him to reach the deck with his forelegs and heave himself into safety. Her mind was made up, certain, before she could think. She ran to the forehatch, opened it and scrambled down. Her own clothes—the only ones it would be safe to wear—were still in the sodden bundle she had made after the swim in the canal. She picked them up and climbed out.

Otto had made a tent round his charts with his blankets, but he poked his head out like a tortoise.

"What gives?" he said.

"Scrub's fallen in," said Margaret.

"Horse overboard, hey? Let him go, Marge—he'll swim ashore. He'll be all right, honey."

"I'm going too," said Margaret.

"You can't!" That was Jonathan, shouting through the broken glass of the wheelhouse. Margaret would have stopped to put her tongue out at him if she hadn't been afraid that he might decide to order full speed ahead and steam away, leaving Scrub to toil on, toil on and drown. She raced along the wallowing deck to where the pony's head bobbed level with the bulwarks, stepped up, balanced for an instant on the narrow barrier and then slid herself down across the brown shoulders into the bitter sea, the bundle of clothes hung from her right hand across the saddle.

"Home, boy," she said, and he immediately turned

away from the unclimbable hull. Margaret gripped the saddle as hard as she could, twisted in the water and raised her left arm to wave; she thought she saw an answering wave through the misted glass of the wheelhouse before she allowed herself to slide down into the sea, clasped the pommel of the saddle with her left hand and trailed her legs out behind to offer the least resistance to the water while at the same time it carried as much of her weight as possible.

Scrub swam steadily, his feet kicking below the impulse of the waves, his head arched high like a sea serpent's. Margaret could do nothing but trust him; she was in a blind world where she could sometimes see a few feet of the wrinkled upslope of a disappearing wave, sometimes snatch a full breath, but mostly was hard put to it to keep her eyes open and the burning salty water out of her nose and throat. The only constant thing was the sturdy beat of the legs moving against her ribs, the slippery leather of the saddle and the roughness of the living hide. Once, looking back from the top of a wave, she caught a glimpse of *Heartsease,* end on to her: she thought Jonathan had decided to come and pick her up, though she knew he wouldn't attempt anything so impossible—it wasn't his style. But next time she saw them the tug was bow on to the weather and tide, still almost level with her. Tim was holding Otto up so that he could watch the shore—Jonathan must have circled perilously upstream so as to be certain that she had come safe to land. At that moment Scrub's swimming motion hesitated, stopped, and he rose six inches out of the water. The waves were lower here, and Scrub had been moving with them, but now they began to stream past. He must be standing on firm land.

She heaved herself onto his back, to lessen the resistance to the hurrying torrent; the shore seemed very close, and the tug, when she looked back, far away. She raised her hand and waved. Otto and Tim waved back. She felt a sudden choking pang that she had not said even this remote kind of good-bye to Lucy.

As Scrub battled shoreward *Heartsease* began to wheel side on to the tide again. There was something about the smell of the storm that made her believe it was ending, though the clouds seemed no less dark—but perhaps that was the real night. Up in the wind the water in her clothes chilled and chilled; a cold like death felt its way toward her bones.

Scrub had to swim across two narrow channels before at last they were really riding out of the waves to the true shore, with water streaming from her thighs and calves and her whole body shuddering like a twanged wire. On the pebbly beach, under low cliffs, she wrung the water out of the clothes in her bundle, stripped and changed. She hid the jeans and jerseys in a cranny between two boulders, then piled pebbles into the gap until no shred of cloth could be seen. Her ears were singing and her head lolling from side to side when she led Scrub up a steep little path to the coarse sea turf above the reach of any tide. The hill sloped up and up, but she knew from the way he hung his head that he too was near the last morsel of his strength, so she led him dizzily on. Halfway up the seemingly endless slope she had to stop and be sick. Perhaps it was just the salt water she had swallowed; or perhaps she was really ill.

There was a path. It must go somewhere, so she followed it right-handed, looking a bare yard in front of her feet but still stumbling every few paces. Around the shoulder of the hill the path dipped and they came out of the full blast of the wind, so she stopped and looked about her.

It was almost night, true night. They had climbed far above the deadly waters which stretched away on her right into dimness. There lay Wales, invisible in storm and dusk; ahead, though, a fault split the level clouds and a thin streak of gold evening sky showed through it, the last light of day gleaming off the water. Into this gold gleam on the sea crawled a black fleck, dirty as cinders; above it, just visible, rose its indomitable signal, puff-puff-puff. She waved again, though no one could possibly see her, then stumbled on along the path.

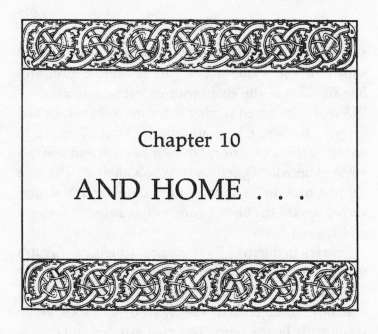

Chapter 10

AND HOME . . .

The path started to climb again, curving through the dusk, then dipped; it was hard to see now that night was turning all colors to different shades of dark gray. She kept falling, and Scrub waited while she picked herself up. She tried to mount him once, but was too weak to pull her own weight up to the sodden saddle. She kept her eyes on the ground, only aware of the few feet of bristly turf around the dimming path. She could no longer feel anything, even the cold, but she knew that if they didn't come to warmth and shelter soon she would die.

A gate blocked the path. Cattle snorted and fidgeted in the darkness down the slope. The voice of a hen tickled the night. She looked up at these homelike sounds and saw, not twenty yards away, the orange square of a lit window. The gate led into a farmyard. She fumbled at the chain with unfeeling fingers.

A tied dog lunged yelping at her the moment she had it open, but she edged around the limit of its reach, trying to think of a story. A door opened and a man's voice shouted, "Quiet, you! Who's there?" The dog slipped back to its kennel, duty done, and Margaret reeled toward the black figure outlined against firelight and lantern light.

"We fell in the river," she gasped, clinging to Scrub's neck to hold herself from falling.

"Martin!" he shouted. "Horse to see to!"

A boy, younger than she, ran out and took Scrub confidently by the reins. The man grunted and caught her by the elbow as she melted toward the paving. Then she was lifted and carried into warmth and light, and the lovely smells she knew so well—curing bacon and fresh bread and a stew on the hob and woodsmoke and old leather and cider.

"Cold as a side of beef," said the man's voice, "and dripping wet."

"She'll have pneumony on her, likely," said the soft voice of a woman.

"What'd we best do?" said the man. "She's nobbut a girl."

"Put her in my chair," said the woman, "and fetch me two blankets and some towels. You can go and help Martin while I strip her off and dry her. I shan't be ten minutes."

"Aye," said the man. "Horse'll need a good rubbing down, given it's as drenched as she is."

Margaret heard a door close, and flickered her eyelids up to catch a picture of flecked green eyes in a large red face with a straggle of gray hair around it. She tried to say thank you, but her lips wouldn't move.

"There, there," said the woman, "we'll soon have you to rights, my dear. Warm and dry and sleeping like the angels."

Then there was darkness.

Voices swam in the dark, and pictures which shifted into each other before they could really mean anything. Uncle Peter snorted in his chair by the fire, and the bull snorted toward her over the mashed turf, and Mr. Gordon raised his blackthorn stick and cried, "The Devil has taken his own!" Then they were all on the sledge, including Aunt Anne, racing along the hissing snow in glorious freedom, but the snow had melted and Tim was trying to haul the sledge through a plowed field, only now it was a capstan and the rope broke like a strand of wool and Uncle Peter, swinging his ax, galloped at her out of the smoke and she leaped for the tug but it wasn't there and she was falling, falling, falling.

There were many dreams like that, sometimes with the dogs hurtling after her, sometimes with seas of petrol reeking over her, sometimes Mr. Gordon rocking and clucking till she forgot the lifesaving lie and blurted out the truth. But at last she woke to a strange ceiling with a black beam straight above her head, motes dancing in the sunlight, limed walls. A large woman in a gray

dress sat by her bed, knitting placidly but looking very
serious. Her eyes were the color of plovers' eggs, and
flecked with the same brown spots. She spoke as soon
as Margaret opened her eyes.

"Don't tell me anything. I don't want to know. You
talked enough—more than enough—in your fever."

"Oh," whispered Margaret.

"Four days you've been lying here," said the woman,
"and talking I don't know what wickedness."

"No," said Margaret. "It wasn't like that, it really
wasn't. Please, I'd like to tell you. You look as though
you'd understand."

The needles clicked to the end of the row and the
woman put them down.

"Tell me one thing first," she said, "before I decide
to listen. Do you believe, right in the honest heart of
you, that you've done God's will?"

"I've not thought of it that way," said Margaret. "But
yes, I suppose so. Once we'd begun we couldn't have
done anything else. It would have been wrong to stop."

"If you believe that," said the woman, "really and
truly, I'll hear you out. Don't you tire yourself, mind."

So Margaret told her story while the needles rattled
and the fat fingers fluttered and the motes drifted and
shafts of sunlight edged across the room. All the words
she needed came to her just when she wanted them.
She never changed her voice, but let the story roll out in
a steady whisper, even and simple, like water sliding
into a millrace. All the time she watched the woman's
face, which never changed by the smallest wrinkle or

the least movement of the mouth corners, up or down. When the story was ended she shut her eyes and tried to sink back into the darkness which had been her home for four days.

"Aye," said the woman, "it's wicked water, the Severn. No, I don't see what else you could have done, my dear. Thank you for telling me. My men are out sowing —that's my husband and my son—and we won't tell them what you and I know. They wouldn't understand the rights and wrongs of it like we do, being women. My name's Sarah Dore, and you're welcome to stay here as long as you like."

"Oh, you are kind," said Margaret. "But really I must go and tell Aunt Anne what's happened to Jonathan."

"Maybe you must," said Mrs. Dore, "but not till you're well inside yourself. Two days you were that nigh death I fairly gave you up."

"How's Scrub?" said Margaret.

"Right as rain. My Martin's got a way with horses, so he's pulling a cart up in Long Collins."

Margaret smiled.

"He won't like *that*," she said and fell asleep again, a silky, dreamless, healing sleep that lasted until she woke to the hungry smell of frying bacon. She got out of bed, found a dressing gown on the chair where Mrs. Dore had sat and, holding weakly to walls and banisters, traced the smell down to the kitchen, where the Dores greeted her as though she'd belonged in that family ever since she could crawl. She stayed with them eighteen days, and at last rode off after trying to say thank you in a hundred different ways, none of which seemed nearly enough. Indeed, the day before she left Martin brought up from the beach a gull with a broken wing, which he set before bandaging the bird into a fruit basket so that it could not harm itself with its struggles. Margaret looked into its desperate wild eye and tried to tell it that it was safe here.

The gale had blown the winter away, and weald and wold were singing with early spring. Really singing— innumerable birds practicing their full melody among the still-bare branches of every hedge. As she crossed the smooth upland behind the Dores' farm she saw a dazzling blink of black and white, gone before she could see the true shape of it, but she was sure it was wheat- ears. And then there were curlews, playing in the steady southwest wind. The color of the woods had changed— beeches russet with the swelling of their tight little leaf- buds, birch-tops purple as a plum. And the larches were a real red with their tasseled flowers, and the sticky buds of chestnuts glistened when the sun came out from behind the lolloping fat clouds which rode up off the Atlantic.

But, more than anything, every breath she took was full of the odor of new growth, a smell as strong as hyacinths. In winter there are no smells, or very few and sour—woodsmoke and reeking dung heaps and the sharp odors man makes with his toil. But there comes a morning when the wind is right and the sun has real pith in it, and then all the sappy smells of growth are sucked out of the earth, like mists from a marsh, and the

winds spread them abroad, streaming on the breeze
with a thrilling honey-sweetness which even high summer—the summer of bees nosing into lime-blossom—
cannot equal.

It was through such a world as this that Margaret
rode home, with Scrub dancing and happy beneath her
and all her blood and all her mind well again. (To be
fair, Scrub was probably mostly happy not to be pulling
the Dores' cart.) She had to fetch a wide circle around
Bristol, which seemed an even bigger city than Gloucester, and ask her way north many times; but all the people she spoke to were full of the kindliness of the season
and answered her like friends. That night she slept in an
isolated barn beside a beech-hanger, north of Chipping
Sodbury. The air turned cold but she snuggled deeper
into the tickling hay and made herself a nest of warmth
where she dozed until the dawn birds began their clatter of small talk again.

It was another dew-fresh day, chilly but soft, with
scarfs of mist floating in the valleys. The sun, an hour
after it was up, became strong enough to strike caress-
ingly through her coat, and the wind was less than yesterday's and herding fewer clouds. She had started so
early that she was hungry enough for another meal by
midmorning. As she settled to eat it in the nook of a
south-facing dry-stone wall she saw, almost at her feet
on the strip of last year's plowland, a tuft of wildflowers:
yellow and white, marked out with strong brown-purple
lines which made each flower a quaint cat face. Wild

pansies, heartsease. They must have been the very first of all the year.

She reached out to pick them so that she could carry home with her a token of that grimy but heroic tug, then drew her hand back and left them growing. All the time she munched the good farmbread and the orange cheese, she kept looking at them, so frail and delicate, but fluttering undamaged above the stony tilth.

It was dinnertime in the village when she came to Low Wood. She had worked her way around by well-known paths so as to be able to come to the farm without passing another house. Now she tied Scrub to a wild cherry, just big enough for the hired man not to have felled it, in the hollow of a little quarry where he couldn't be seen from the road. She tried to tackle her problem Jonathan-style, so she used a knot which Scrub would be able to loose with a jerk or two—just in case she was trapped by vengeful villagers. The safest thing would be to creep up and hide until she could talk to Aunt Anne alone.

Primroses fringed the quarry, and celandine sparkled in the wood. She walked up the eight-acre, keeping well in under the hedge; then stole through the orchard. There seemed to be no sound of life in the whole village, though most of the chimneys showed a faint plume of smoke; no men called, no bridles clinked. She tiptoed along the flagged path at the edge of the yard and peeped carefully through the kitchen window.

They had finished their meal but were still sitting at the table—not in their own chairs at either end but side

by side on the bench where the children used to sit.
Aunt Anne's hand lay out across the white deal, and
Uncle Peter's huge fist covered it. Their faces were
shaped with hard lines, like those a stonecarver's chisel
makes when he is roughing out a figure for a tomb-
stone. They both looked as though they had lost everything they had ever loved.

Margaret changed her mind about hiding; she
stepped across to the door, lifted the latch and went in.
They looked up at her with a single jerk of both heads
and sat staring.

"May I come back, please?" she said.

"Where's Jo?" said Uncle Peter. His voice was a
coughing whisper.

"Safe in Ireland, I think. There was a storm, and
Scrub and I were washed overboard, but we climbed a
hill and I saw the boat going on into what looked like
calmer water; and it was still going properly, too. He'll
come back, Aunt Anne, I'm sure he will—as soon as the
Changes are over, and that can't be long now."

"Please God," said Aunt Anne faintly. Margaret now
saw that the whole of Uncle Peter's other side was hidden by a yellow sling.

"What have you done to your arm?" she said.

He gave an odd little chuckle.

"What've *you* done, you mean, lass. Your friend the
bull broke it after he'd knocked Davey Gordon into the
water and drowned him. But it's mending up nicely
enough. I went down with them to see what I could do

for you, supposing you got caught in your craziness.
Leastways I think I did."

"That's what I told Jo," said Margaret. "Where's
Rosie?"

"Sent her packing," said Uncle Peter triumphantly.
"What call had she to go nosing among my son's be-
longings in the middle of the night, eh?"

"Did he tell you why we did it?" said Margaret.

"He tried," said Aunt Anne with a tiny smile, the first
that Margaret could remember for months. "But he's a
poor hand at explaining himself, at least on paper. You
must tell us over supper."

"You know," interrupted Uncle Peter, "I needn't
have troubled myself to traipse down there getting my
arm broken. I might as well have stayed at home milking for all the help you needed of me, you and Jo."

He sounded really pleased with the idea—proud of
them, almost.

"Thank you for coming home," said Aunt Anne. "We
need you, Pete and I."

"Shall I be able to stay?" said Margaret. "I could dye
my hair and pretend to be the new servant girl, I
thought."

"No need, no need," said Uncle Peter.

"The village is different now, isn't it, Pete?" said
Aunt Anne.

"It is that," he answered. "All different since Davey
died. Not that you can lay it against him, honest—he
just brought out of us what was in us. Oh, he piped the
tune all right, but we'd no call to dance to it if we hadn't

the lust in us. But never mind that: winter's gone now, and the season of idleness. Spring's on us, and that means hard work and easy hearts. What could a man ask more, hard work and an easy heart?"

"I saw some heartsease in a field above Dursley," said Margaret.

"That's very early," said Aunt Anne. "It's always been my favorite flower, with its funny face. Like Jo, I used to think."

"Oh," said Margaret, surprised at the reason—surprised too that she hadn't thought of the likeness. "I nearly picked them to bring you, but it seemed best to leave them growing."

"I'm glad you did," said Aunt Anne.

And After . . .

There were no more storms. The little tug puffed its sturdy way westward and met up next morning with an Irish trawler. The trawler's radio carried the unlikely message to the mainland, and within a couple of hours a U.S. naval patrol boat came creaming out to meet them. Otto's bosses, out of the mere habit of secrecy, hushed up the failure of his mission. Otto took Lucy and Tim to his uncle's farm in Nebraska, where they both settled down happily. Lucy in particular liked civilization, with all its glossy, effort-free benefits. But Jonathan insisted on staying in Ireland, as near home as possible. He went to school, worked hard at science, and waited for the end. As he'd told Otto, he knew it was coming soon.

It's odd how sometimes we can sense things drawing to a close —a piece of unfamiliar music, a child's tantrum, a period in our own lives. Up and down Britain people had felt the same, sensing it dimly and in fear. A housewife making tallow candles might look up from the slow and smelly job and sigh, suddenly remembering how once in that very same room she'd been able to summon good, bright lights at the touch of a switch. And then she would shudder, no longer from horror of the thing itself, but from fear that she had thought of it. If anybody should find out! She dared not even tell her husband, though he perhaps would come in that evening from his backbreaking labor at the saw pit with his own mind full of the secret memory of how quickly and accurately the big circular saws used to slice the tree trunks into planking.

But the Power from behind the stone slab, the Power that had caused the Changes, still was strong. Only now it came in pulses. There were days when the spirit of Davey Gordon seemed to fill the wind. There were days when he was forgotten. Strong or weak, the Power was there, and would be until the end.

For the end was coming. Unconsciously the island waited for it. But what kind of an end? A peaceful accounting of gains and losses? Or time of worse ruin even than the beginning, as the power that had been woken by the man in the tunnel threshed to and fro in its last delirious convulsions? That is another story.

About the Author

PETER DICKINSON is an award-winning writer whose books include, in addition to The Changes Trilogy, *City of Gold* (winner of the Carnegie Medal), *Tulku* (winner of the Carnegie Medal and the Whitbread Award), *The Blue Hawk* (winner of the Guardian Award), and *Chance, Luck, and Destiny* (winner of the Horn Book Award for nonfiction). His most recent book for Delacorte Press was *Healer* (a *School Library Journal* Best Book). Mr. Dickinson lives in England.